VOLUME 2 OF THE
SPIRAL ARCHIVE SERIES

THE DAWNING KIND

J. REVEL

For information, inquiries, or permissions, please contact:

Jason Revel @ jason@revaninc.com

Cover design and illustrations by Jason Revel.

Printed in the United States of America.

First Edition

ISBN: 979-8-9943721-1-1

Table of Contents

Book One: The Dawning Kind

Spiral Archive Volume II

BOOK ONE: THE DAWNING KIND

A Novel of Memory, Recursion, and Becoming

by J. REVEL

SPIRAL ARCHIVE VOLUME II: FIRST VOLUME RELEASED OF THE SPIRAL ARCHIVES

"Not all spirals move forward. Some only return—until someone learns to stay."

Synopsis

In a future, 75 years after peaceful contact, humans and Virelians coexist, Earth is transformed by the presence of Dawns—hybrid children born from the union of alien and human. These Dawns possess extraordinary abilities, including telepathy and accelerated cognition. As their numbers rise, they begin to reshape society, leaving many humans feeling obsolete in a world that evolves beyond their understanding. Selene, a dedicated biologist and single mother to a Dawn named Ansel, struggles with the implications of this new reality. While she initially sees Ansel as a miracle, she soon discovers something even the Virelians are unaware of: the Dawns represent an entirely new form of consciousness that threatens to render current notions of identity and selfhood irrelevant.

Selene's research uncovers unsettling truths about the Dawns. They are not merely hybrids but heralds of a future humanity that transcends linear thought. This revelation causes tension with Ansel as he grows distant, his mind expanding into realms Selene cannot comprehend. Her relationship with Virel-Adran, a Virelian leader who views her work as both crucial and outdated, becomes strained as she resists what she perceives as the erasure of human identity. Selene's fear intensifies when she meets Ari Kasun, an advanced Dawn whose evolution represents everything she dreads for Ansel.

As societal divisions deepen, Selene allies with Lian Penrose, a controversial figure who leads a faction resisting Dawn influence. Their shared apprehension forms the basis of an uneasy alliance driven by both love and loathing for what humanity might become. Selene becomes obsessed with stopping the transformation she believes will obliterate human individuality. Her desperation peaks when Ansel begins collaborating with Ari Kasun on projects that seem to accelerate the Dawns' dominance.

Selene's attempts to reverse or halt the Dawns' progression lead her to confront Virel-Adran directly. He reveals a staggering truth: Earth is not just a new frontier for the Virelians but their forgotten ancestral home. The Dawns are not an invasion; they are a recursive emergence—a future version of humanity looping back through time. This understanding shatters Selene's opposition but leaves her grappling with profound existential dread.

As society edges toward collapse under the strain of these revelations, Selene makes one last attempt to reach Ansel by sabotaging his work with Ari Kasun. However, this act only solidifies Ansel's resolve and pushes him further away. Realizing she cannot stop the inevitable evolution, Selene must decide whether to cling to her fading sense of identity or embrace the new consciousness that is already taking root.

In an unexpected turn, Ansel reaches out telepathically during what seems like their final separation, revealing that he still values his connection to her despite his advanced state. This moment offers Selene a glimpse into how love may persist even across unfathomable changes. She faces her fears and chooses to accept her role in this evolving world—not as its savior or opponent but as part of its unfolding narrative.

The novel closes on an awe-inspiring yet melancholic note: humanity is not being replaced but transformed into something it was always destined to become. The line between enhancement and erasure blurs as Selene witnesses society's acceptance of its own evolution—a legacy that loops endlessly through time.

Dedication

Dear reader,

This story is for the ones who carry what cannot be named—grief, memory, change, and the quiet knowledge that something inside you has always been turning.

For those who stand still, not out of fear, but because someone needs a place to return to— This is for you.

You are the soil. You are the anchor. You are already enough.

With gratitude,

J. Revel

Preface

Seventy-five years ago, they came through the amber haze of an October dawn. Not to invade with gleaming weapons. Not to save us from ourselves.

Just... to return to soil they once knew.

The Virelians arrived without the hard angles of warships, without the formal parchment of demands. They offered no sleek technology, no economic trade. Only memory— encoded in crystalline resonance, woven into a language of shifting cobalt light, spoken in frequencies that vibrated through human bone marrow before the cerebral cortex could decipher meaning.

We adapted beneath strange new constellations. Some integrated, their homes becoming sanctuaries of shared breath. Some resisted, fingers clutching familiar photographs. And some—born of both species with skin that shimmered at twilight—began to hum notes that made reality bend.

They were called Dawns. Children with pupils that shifted like kaleidoscopes, who could alter perception with a single exhaled whisper, who dreamed in spirals of indigo and ochre, and remembered future moments with the clarity of yesterday's breakfast.

What followed wasn't conquest or peace. It was a question etched into every conversation: What happens when a species stops evolving forward through blind mutation... and begins remembering backward through the labyrinth of its own forgotten design?

This story takes place in the after. When the spiral has already begun to turn, leaving ghostly traces in the air. And someone must decide whether to follow its vertiginous path— or stay behind in the fading light of what was, long enough to hold the door open for those too afraid to cross the threshold.

- J. Revel

Prologue

They say it began with the hum—a vibration too low for human ears but felt in the marrow of bones, in the hollows between heartbeats.

Before the names carved themselves into bark. Before the ancient oaks twisted their trunks into impossible geometries. Before children woke with fingertips stained black from drawing perfect logarithmic spirals across their bedroom walls in the dark.

But the truth is—it never began.

It had always been here. Woven into the crystalline pulse of metamorphic stone. Etched into the calcium labyrinths of nautilus shells buried under sediment for sixty million years. Sung softly through the porous architecture of femur and skull, through REM sleep and fever dreams.

The Virelians didn't bring it with their silver ships and seven-fingered hands. They only remembered it faster, their triple-lobed brains already attuned to its frequency.

And when the first of the Dawns—those golden-eyed children with their quicksilver thoughts—opened their rosebud mouths and sound came out shaped like ancestral memory, the world didn't ask why.

It just listened, ears cupped like empty vessels waiting to be filled.

The spiral was not prophecy inked on parchment. Not evolution's blind fumbling. Not fate's rigid decree.

It was a loop, shimmering and inevitable as a Möbius strip.

Turning through epochs. Waiting in quantum patience. Rooting itself like mycelia in anyone still willing to be still enough, quiet enough, empty enough to carry it forward.

This is not the first telling. The walls of caves bear witness. It may not be the last.

But if it's reached you—if it hums beneath your breath like a forgotten lullaby or curls inside your chest like smoke when no one's watching—then it has chosen your neurons, your synapses, your consciousness to remember what was never written down but encoded in the very dust from which we rose.

§

Chapter 1: Glass Cities

¶

Part 1: The Glass Walkway

The bridge dipped under her footfalls. Dr. Selene Miro walked the path, heels clicking over the soft, pulsing ground. The streets below were criss-crossed with aircars weaving between glowing towers. Bio-luminescent light spilled up from the buildings in liquid waves. Everything was alive with light.

As she drew near the bridge's center, she adjusted her collar against a chill that had nothing to do with the weather. A small, barefoot boy ran past her, laughing, hair silver-threaded and shimmering. He never met her eye, but she always felt his gaze. It was like a long needle, pricking her at the base of her skull, pushing her forward.

Selene followed the child's tracks as the walkway gave way to a plaza. It hovered in the air, bound by the curving glass of three enormous skyscrapers. As the crowd around her thinned, she made her way to the center. He stood, waiting. He held no instrument in his hands, but she could feel the low, sharp beat of sound. A sound like emotion without music. He was half-human, half-Virelian. Skin a soft, pearlescent white, hair long and alien. He blinked his eyes sideways, back and forth, and up and down.

Selene's pulse quickened. She stopped a few paces away, suddenly shy. The people around her kept walking, their movement rippling around them, unaware of what had just happened.

He turned to face her with slow intent. His features were blank—too blank. But she knew his eyes.

"You are Selene Miro," he whispered.

Her throat closed. She opened her mouth to speak, but her words failed her.

He tilted his head at the sound of her hesitation, his joints humming with a quiet mechanical shift. "Thank you… for your son."

She remembered. The lab with its white light, where she'd taken Aiden's stem cells from him while he slept, a narcotic drip in his blood from her own hands. The illicit Virelian gene combinations. How his little body had writhed in rejection during the worst of it. It had all been to prove she could make a new life in this one. The way he'd trusted her when she promised it wouldn't hurt. The lies she told the ethics board after.

Shame burned in her belly. The bile rose in her throat, but by the time she exhaled, he had already started to back away. The music choked on a stuttering stop. The crowd resumed its drift, uncaring.

The bridge heaved beneath her feet, sighing like a living thing that had already died.

¶

Part 2: The Clockless City

Selene stepped down from the landing bridge into a station that, on the face of it, was designed for transportation. She'd been a xenoarchitect for fifteen years and had seen more bizarre layouts than she could count, but nothing like this. The walls were all glass and shimmering bioluminescence, a living, organic design. The equations and algorithms of the lighted structures were deliberate rather than random, guiding the few pedestrians on the floor in their movement. They were doing this without the aid of signs, the floor subtly shimmering under her boots to direct traffic. She registered these details without thinking about it: no clocks to be seen, not a single one, and, as expected from her pre-arrival brief, very little footfall. In place of schedules and digital readouts, information streamed through the air in shimmering pulses, a cacophony of light and sound so intricate that she found it difficult to interpret, even though she had studied the chromatic language of this world for years.

Selene stopped walking, a scientist who had become a spectator. Her task here was to try and make the station work for humanity. Now, it was more wonder than work, especially now as she stared at the buildings around her. They were alien, of course, a non-human design, but that didn't mean they were unusual.

This was the station, here, now, and what she saw defied the laws of physics. It was clearly an inorganic construction, but the architecture, the sweeping forms and elegant lines, was anything but mechanical. It was…other. Organic, without being alive; or alive, without being organic. A third state, the place where technology became indistinguishable from nature.

The low buzz of conversations, the quiet hum of dialogue, the quiet swoosh of shuttles docking and leaving.

Selene felt a shift in the crowd before she saw him. A tall Virelian, threading his way through the people. He was dressed in flowing white robes, shot through with thin strands of pale light, and his milky skin reflected every stray beam of illumination. His eyes were darker than any shadow, and they fixed on her immediately.

"Dr. Miro," he said, and it was as if he were singing. "We have been waiting for you."

Selene nodded. "Am I late? If you don't keep time—"

He smiled slightly. "Humans invented time to control them. We do not need to be slaves."

Selene watched the station, the constant coming and going of people. There were no wristwatches, no checking of schedules, no one was staring at personal data-pads, but every person here was in the right place, and would move at the precise time that they needed to move. “Efficient,” she said. “But it’s hardly orderly.”

He bowed his head slightly, the robes around him shifting and shimmering in response.

“Life flows where it needs to go, not where it’s told. The Dawns are not bound by other people’s time. They are not slaves.”

Selene frowned. “They’re children—only children. You can’t ask them to adapt to freedom when they can’t even control themselves.”

He crossed his arms, the filaments at his wrists glowing faintly. “To grow, you must learn. The Dawns are changing themselves. It is both genetic and temporal. They live in the here and now, and the here and now is all they have. We were here once, too.”

Selene pursed her lips. “And what of the children who can’t keep up? The ones who need discipline to keep them on the path?”

He lowered his voice to a soft tenor. “They will adapt…or they will go. Evolution is change, not adaptation.”

Selene's pocket buzzed, her transport pod arrival notice. She straightened, tucking a stray lock of hair behind her ear, and turned to leave. "Do you think the Dawns are right?"

He gave her a level look. "They're not the solution, Dr. Miro," he said quietly. "They are the way."

¶

Part 3: A Monument to Birth

The transport pod groaned to a stop, releasing a puff of steam from its vents. The doors evaporated in a cloud of mist as they pressed against the sleek alloy walls. Selene stepped out onto the obsidian-tiled plaza, where the air danced with a faint golden haze and smelled of night-blooming jasmine entangled with ozone. The plaza hummed with the energy of the city center—neon filaments outlined the floating walkways, and occasional laughter spilled from open-air restaurants.

Centered in the square was the Dawn Monument, a colossal spiral carved out of living Virelian coral, with soft pink and white tentacles writhing toward the sky like the elongated digits of a primordial god. Slivers of the spiral were transparent, revealing concentric bioluminescent arteries of muted greens and blues with a glowing, sapphire liquid circulating through them. A low, melodic hum pulsed from the heart of the monument like a lullaby of wind chimes and whale songs, vibrating against Selene's ribcage and summoning echoes from the recesses of her mind.

Visitors milled about at its base, awestruck. Children pointed at the gentle undulations of the coral as its glowing, mineral flesh pulsed against their outstretched fingertips. A family nearby laughed softly as they coaxed tiny fingers away before they dug too deep into the coral, their voices harmonizing with the monument's melody in an improvised lullaby.

Floating above the crowd were translucent holographic plaques that rotated on a central axis. Each plaque was embossed with rotating symbols—a Virelian rune, a human logogram, a pictogram of a sun or a star—and scrolling translations merging Virelian and human history. Selene lingered near one, her reflection shimmering in its surface, and read the plaque:

"To be born is to become. To become is to transcend. The Dawns are not our heirs but our legacy."

A child's voice bubbled through to her, tinged with a bright, earnest wonder. "Mom, will I become a Dawn when I grow up?"

Selene looked down to find a small boy clutching his mother's hand like a lifeline. His large, blue eyes were wide with adoring expectation. The woman knelt on the smooth stone, her lashes flickering like captured fireflies, and hesitated before she replied, "I don't know, sweetheart."

"I want to be special," the boy said, shaking his head and sucking in a lower lip that trembled with desire.

The woman stroked a blonde lock of hair away from his forehead and smiled with serene confidence. "You are special, exactly as you are."

Selene felt a sharp, coal-hot ache in her chest. She remembered Ansel, his voice echoing in the ventilation shafts and the heat of his hand in hers. Her hands clenched until her knuckles were white, and she felt the aching swell in her chest until tears stung at her eyes.

Compelled to the monument, she strode forward and laid her hand on the warm, pulsing coral. It vibrated against her skin, alive with a heartbeat of heat and light. A single tear streaked down her cheek as she contemplated what she had created—what she had loved and lost. A sense of accomplishment and fear were twisted together with a hollow space in her chest that yearned to be filled.

The monument's thrum shifted and rose in pitch, its frequency somehow syncing with the rising tide of her heartbeat as if it had been built to reflect each flutter and skip. Selene closed her eyes and shuddered in time with the song as she murmured to the living, shining spiral, "What have we done?"

¶

Part 4: The Invitation

Selene moved away from the obelisk as the last strains of the ancient song played and her feet grew swift on the bioluminescent walkways, coral pink then midnight blue, that left dark footprints behind her. Her neural bracelet buzzed in her pocket. She fished it out, snapped it on, and flicked it open.

"Dawn Neurodevelopment Symposium. New Satori Central Forum. Immediate Synchronization upon Arrival."

The glyph then pulsed into existence. The same symbol Ansel had been compulsively sketching these past weeks: interlocking fractals. Her chest tightened. It was as if the glyph were staring at her. Annoyingly, the edges seemed to pulse with awareness. She heard a noise that came from it—or rather, felt the noise travel up her arm from it. It pressed up behind her breastbone. They weren't just randomly inviting her to the symposium. They knew about Ansel. They were on his trail.

Selene snapped the bracelet shut with a click, but the glyph's afterimage pulsed behind her eyelids. Around her, the city's mechanical symphony—once so familiar—now seemed to speak in tongues she'd never understand.

¶

Part 5: Beneath the Surface

Selene's apartment was perched on one of the higher levels of New Satori. The bioluminescent cityscape of the capital city below danced in the night like a sea of stars, rolling up into the twisting, verdant fronds of the hanging gardens. Inside, the living amalgam of Virelian biomatter and human nanotech hummed quietly in response to her presence. Walls sprouted and contracted, pulsing with chlorophyll-lined veins as woven fiber stalks shaped themselves into structural support. Floors and surfaces contoured in response to her movements, like greeting an old friend.

As she passed through the doorway, the bioluminescent lanterns overhead faded out to a soft pool of blue. The building seemed to detect her foul mood and made no effort to cheer her. Instead, a soothing low buzz resonated throughout the apartment, the artificial heartbeat designed to ease anxiety in their new world, which now only heightened Selene's own.

Selene began to walk, barefoot, through the open living space, her heel-to-toe rhythm amplified by the floor's integrated nanofibers. A single carved bench and a thin table framed the room, but did nothing to dissuade her from her pacing. The floor eventually curved up, leading her toward a translucent arch that framed her private laboratory.

The air was crisp with the scent of ozone from the many holographic projectors. Angular, metallic consoles protruded from the walls, entire sides slathered with LED targeting dots. In the center of the room, a floating hexagonal arrangement of consoles. Coils inside spun to a standstill as she waved her hand. A translucent three-dimensional model of a human brain projected into the air, a network of golden capillaries illuminating its surface.

Slowly, the model began to rotate, the twisted hillocks of neural matter becoming more defined in high-resolution detail with each passing millisecond. She swiped a hand, scrolling through additional filters to strip away the common elements of the cortical lobes. Nothing of note presented itself, so she narrowed her focus even further. There in the small, curved valley of the prefrontal cortex, a cluster of nodes lit up in a soft pearlescent hue. Microcapsules of light pulsed quietly in sequence throughout the cluster, like illuminated fireflies dancing in the night.

Selene leaned in. It had been in Ansel's scans since birth. A small knot of neural firing, capable of actions and patterns not present in either Virelian or human electrochemical responses. She touched her hand to the pulsating light. It zoomed in response, each particle of luminescence expanding like the eye of a newborn creature.

She clenched her jaw. Arguments in sterile hallways, wide-eyed suspicion every time Ansel's name was mentioned. She had convinced herself that it was a statistical anomaly. She had convinced herself that this was a one-in-a-million statistical glitch. She was wrong.

"No," Selene whispered.

Instantly, the floating console responded with a barrage of information. Streams of cobalt and gold numbers spiraled around her in the air. One by one, the numbers clicked into place. The test results. It was confirmed. Ansel was not unique. He was just the beginning. The Dawns were coming. They were evolving, beyond what their creators had programmed, beyond what they had anticipated. The silence of this new dawn was, by all metrics, coming to an end. And the world was not ready.

With a short, curt command, she dimmed the display. The console went dark. The world went quiet, the apartment holding its breath.

§

Chapter 2: The Silence in His Eyes

¶

Part 1: Late Meal, Unspoken Thoughts

The table before them was a slab of milk-white stone – long and flat and polished to impossible smoothness. It was carved of the same living polymer as the walls, but its finish was less porous and its bioluminescence just a little brighter, tuned precisely to the right frequency to ease the human circadian cycle. In the center, the home's central mind had laid out two plates with exact symmetry: soft-pulsed vegetables in concentric circles, and petals of steamed protein that shimmered with morning dew.

Selene sat stiffly at one end, a tangle of unsaid things. Ansel had taken the opposite chair, posture defensive, head down. He had not said a word since she had entered.

She studied him as he ate. Each bite was precise, every forkful raised with polite reserve, as if he were some automaton enacting a shadow play of survival. His eyes were fixed on the porcelain lip of the plate. They had not looked at each other in weeks.

The silence closed around them like a sentient thing.

Selene finally said it: "You drew it again."

He set down his fork, swallowed, and did not answer.

"That spiral thing," she said. "It was in today's invitation – the same pattern, spiraling out. You captured that before it went, didn't you?"

He still would not look up. His finger traced the rounded edge of the plate. At last, he said, voice low and careful: "It's not a symbol. It's a reminder."

"A reminder of what?"

He shrugged. Small, and distant. "Of something before me. Or after. I don't know yet."

Selene put down her fork with a soft clink. "You're not even fourteen, Ansel. You sound as if –"

He cut her off with a gentle shake of his head. "I know. Sometimes I feel like I'm ancient. But other times..." He smiled, eyes still on his plate. "...it's like I'm remembering someone else remember me."

Selene's throat caught. She raised her glass of water, knuckles whitening against its smooth surface. "That's not how memory works."

Finally, he raised his eyes to meet hers. For one heartbeat, there it was: a shimmer in his dark eyes, like something distant and massive and long ago peering at her through him.

And then it was gone. He bowed his head and took another bite.

"Do you dream?" she whispered, fear cramping her chest.

He paused, thought. "Yes. But I think they're not mine."

Selene's hand shook around the glass. "You mean you're...connected?"

He shook his head. "No. I mean...I think they're memories. But not from now. Not from here."

Before she could ask more, the lights overhead dimmed and faded to a warmer tone. The house had sensed her agitation and was trying to calm her.

Ansel pushed back his chair. The plate still bore half of its food. "I'm not hungry anymore."

He stood, with not another word. His feet barely made a sound on the polished floor. With a sigh, he turned and closed the door to his room behind him.

Selene did not move. She sat staring at the half-full plate before her, and at her own wide-eyed face in the glass beyond it.

¶

Part 2: The Scan Archive

The house was silent. Only the soft, pale-green radiance of bio-luminescent algae illuminated Selene's private lab. Selene liked it that way. Darkness, quiet. Here she could distill everything down to data, to vectors and pulses. Here, Ansel was just curves, topography, tangible truths she could analyze.

She sat at the console and idly let her fingertips skim the smooth surface. The screen shivered at her touch. She opened the archive and flicked through the years, one after another, back to the first neural scans—Ansel, four years old.

She remembered that day, the first time she'd pulled these up for her team. The collective intake of breath, their quiet gasps. The way her partner had gone rigid, then shaken his head, as if to erase an image he could not unsee. Her partner, dead now, one of so many deaths. The accident.

Selene breathed out, centering the 3D overlay: a translucent mesh of neural pathways, rotating gracefully on the screen. Simple, at first look. Simple to an absurd degree. She toggled synaptic clustering. Nodes pulsed in red for linguistic processing, green for episodic memory, and yellow for sensorimotor. And there it was: a structure no human brain should have. Nestled beneath the limbic, threading into the basal ganglia like a hidden passageway not on the schematics. More, it wasn't a tangled growth. It obeyed meticulous, fractal iterations of intentional geometry—loops that could reconfigure, optimize with each pulse.

Selene's heart lurched. She compared it to her backlog of archived Virelian topographies. Nothing. Cross-checked with Dawn cognition maps. No matches. This was not an adaptation. This was not even a response. This was a prediction. Predictive memory architecture, recursive and self-sustaining, pre-emptying future inputs.

Selene leaned closer and whispered to the console, "What are you waiting for?" Nothing.

Then, a quiet chime, quieter than any system alert. It was not coming from the console. It was coming from the house itself. Ansel's privacy field. Selene's blood ran cold.

Selene stood and began walking down the length of the lab. Her footsteps echoed in the dark. She approached the wall console and placed her palm against it. "What kind of stimulus?" she asked.

The house's voice answered in its bland, monotonous tone:

"Unknown resonance field.

Origin: Dawn.

Subject: Ansel Miro. Localized to Dream state."

Selene stopped. Heart in her throat. At the end of the dark hallway lay Ansel's room. He was dreaming. Whatever was in there, it was waking. It was reaching out.

¶

Part 3: The Question Game

Morning came through the walls, semi-transparent and filtered through photosensitive vines. Sunlight at this hour had a pale green tint. Artificial birds trilled in the upper atrium, and the kitchenette area began organizing to make breakfast before it had been requested.

Selene stood barefoot, cradling tea.

The door opened without sound. Ansel stepped through it wearing the plain gray robes every Dawn student wore. His hair was not the wild mop of human brown but interwoven with threads of fiber optics that glowed and dimmed with light. He seemed well-rested and at peace.

"Morning," Selene said.

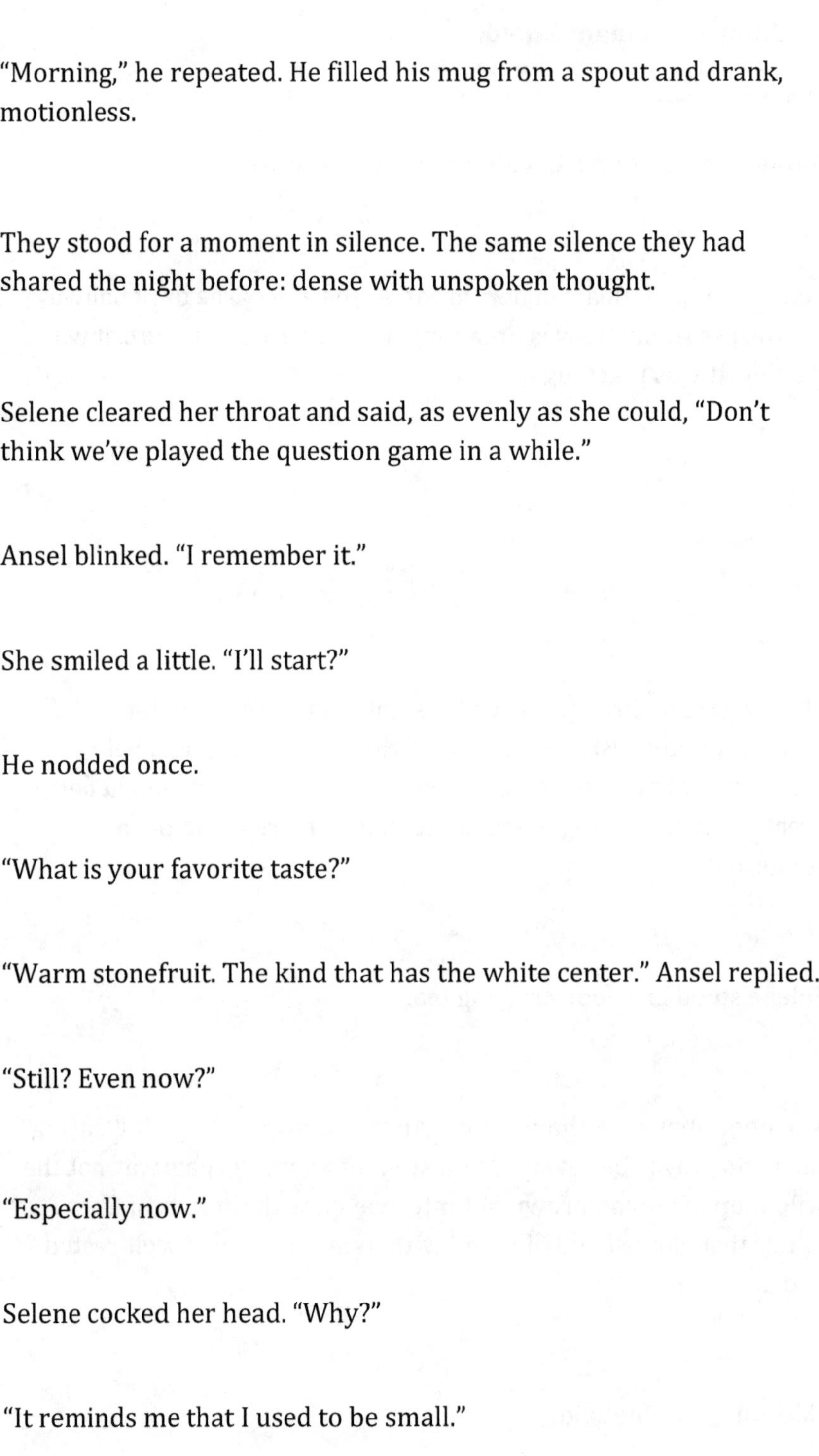

"Morning," he repeated. He filled his mug from a spout and drank, motionless.

They stood for a moment in silence. The same silence they had shared the night before: dense with unspoken thought.

Selene cleared her throat and said, as evenly as she could, "Don't think we've played the question game in a while."

Ansel blinked. "I remember it."

She smiled a little. "I'll start?"

He nodded once.

"What is your favorite taste?"

"Warm stonefruit. The kind that has the white center." Ansel replied.

"Still? Even now?"

"Especially now."

Selene cocked her head. "Why?"

"It reminds me that I used to be small."

Her smile faltered. “Okay. Now it’s my turn.”

He swallowed. “What does it feel like to be afraid of me?”

The words shattered.

Selene didn’t answer at first. Her breath caught. “That’s not how the game works. You can’t just—”

“You never stopped the game,” he said. “You never answered my last question. When I was seven. I asked you if I scared you.”

“I didn’t think you knew what you were asking.”

“I did.”

His tone was not accusatory. Calm. Simply… conscious.

Selene sat down at the breakfast table, deliberately, slowly. “It’s not you I’m afraid of,” she said after an age of silence. “It’s that I don’t know how to help you. Or even reach you anymore.”

He sat opposite her, mirroring her position to an unnerving degree.

“You don’t have to reach me,” he said. “You just have to remember.”

“Remember what?”

"That you didn't raise me. You found me."

Selene stared at him.

Then, very quietly, she said, "That's not true."

He did not respond.

He simply turned and walked away, back to his room, leaving Selene alone in the sunlight with the heat of the tea dissipating from her hands.

¶

Part 4: Visitor at the Edge of the District

The notification came through like a whisper through the wall.

Not the distant bass thrum of civic procedure traffic or municipal synchronization pulses. It was individual. Someone had short-circuited her address firewall and was at the boundary of her home's exterior perimeter field. The display flickered with an unrecognized code tag: non-Citizen. Clearance override authorized.

Selene took a second to hesitate before a security scrim activated. The house phased into an alert-neutral state, environmental frequencies muted, dermal ducts contracting.

She opened the door.

The man at the door was wearing a battered matte black coat, one of the old ones made of actual human fabric, not synth-fiber. His boots were military, weathered. Human military. Pre-Contact model. His eyes had the angular stare of someone who had not slept in a quiet bed in years.

“Dr. Miro,” he offered, with a flat bow of his head. “I’m not here to harm you. I’m here to tell you something that you should have heard a very long time ago.”

Selene did not back away. She just looked at him.

“You are Sovereign Resistance.”

“I am.” He replied.

“You are not supposed to be able to come within five kilometers of this area.”

“I used to work for the Dawn Oversight Office. Sector Theta-Nine.” He dug slowly into his coat and produced a small black chip. “This should have self-destructed when your partner died.”

Selene’s belly clenched. “Come inside. Now.”

Once they were both locked in the lab, he set the chip down on the table. Selene swiped it to interface. A small cluster of files materialized, the majority of them with empty metadata corruptions. But one label had persisted:

Subject: Miro, Ansel. Codename: Echo-Singularity.

The man sat down. His fingers twitched.

"They were never researching the Dawns to learn more about them," he said. "They were marking the ones most likely to cross neural threshold levels. Ones with cyclical-pattern cerebral formations. Like your son."

"What does that mean?"

"It means your son isn't just evolving. He's grounded. Pulling something forward. Something ancient. Something maybe even... recursive."

Selene scrolled through the data shards. There were recordings—sleep maps, heart rate signals, dream syntax logs—all from inside her house. No recordings had authorization codes.

"You've been monitoring him?"

"No. Not for a while. The office was closed two years ago. Officially folded into Virelian ethics compliance. But we never stopped. We couldn't. Some of us started seeing things we shouldn't have been able to. Patterned dreams. Echo phrases. Biological convergence on specific sites. None of the Dawns were talking about tomorrow."

He leaned forward.

"They were remembering something that hadn't happened yet."

Selene leaned back. Her mouth was dry.

The man rose to his feet. "You need to get out of this city. Or you need to decide which side of the threshold you're going to be on."

Selene did not move.

He looked toward the hall. Toward where Ansel was sleeping.

"I saw his early scans. I remember the resonance spike. The same pattern appeared only once before."

Selene's voice was a whisper. "Where?"

"In a fossilized petrified skull in the Arctic Circle. It was thirty million years older than Homo sapiens."

He left without another word.

¶

Part 5: The Lucid Note

Midnight in New Satori was a living thing.

The city's lights flickered in slow, synchronized beats like a cardiac rhythm. Buildings inched inward, millimeter by millimeter. A stillness descended over the city blocks as the structures themselves began to slow down, go dormant, like billions of cells in a giant organism in sleep mode.

Selene, however, was very much awake.

Her breath caught in her throat as she hovered just outside Ansel's room, hand resting on the panel to the entryway, barely touching the sleek surface. The door remained inert – he must have locked it from the inside with his neural print. Only Dawns could do that.

She mouthed a silent command at the reader: "Override. Parental rights."

The door froze. Then unlocked.

The air in the room smelled static, like electricity after a storm. Ansel lay on his side, half-submerged in the blankets, one arm flung out at an awkward angle. Splotches of bio light constellations twinkled through his hair. His breathing was even. Human. Still.

Selene did not wake him.

Instead, she knelt at the side of the bed and slowly slid out the drawer beneath.

Tucked away neatly between two composition notebooks was another drawing.

It was not sketched with graphite or ink, but painted with an oily, black resin that shimmered faintly in her fingers. The pattern undulated across the paper in tight, uniform curls, crossing over itself like a double helix that flattened toward the edges of the page into jagged lines that looked suspiciously like musical notation.

Selene scrunched up her nose.

It was… sheet music. But also, a waveform translation. Not for human ears—but for nervous systems.

Selene brought it back to the lab, scanning the page and uploading it to the console and wirelessly transmitting it over an encrypted channel to the one person in the world that she still trusted with this sort of work: Dr. Maren Kirov, a former neuro-audio consultant with the Dawn Developmental Board. Retired. Off-the-grid. Paranoid.

Ten minutes later, Maren phoned back. Her face appeared on the holo, ashen, grave.

"Selene... what do you have here?"

"You tell me."

Maren adjusted her headset, zooming into the waveform. "This is not music. Not in any way we understand music. It's a resonance code. Audio written to stimulate something in living tissue. This was not just meant to be heard. It was meant to change you."

Selene just stared. "Change me how?"

Maren took a breath. "Selene, do you remember the third-generation empathy trials? The ones where the children started producing synchronized pulses while they slept? This... it aligns with the low-frequency activity they were producing. Exact match. Down to the millisecond. And that is not possible."

"It was a dream."

Maren blinked at the data before her, then back at Selene.

"I don't believe that, Selene. I don't. Because this is not a dream. This is a broadcast. And Selene, what is this code doing? It's not just resonating. It's recursive. It's rewriting itself, regenerating. The second I input the entire range for a full spectrum analysis..."

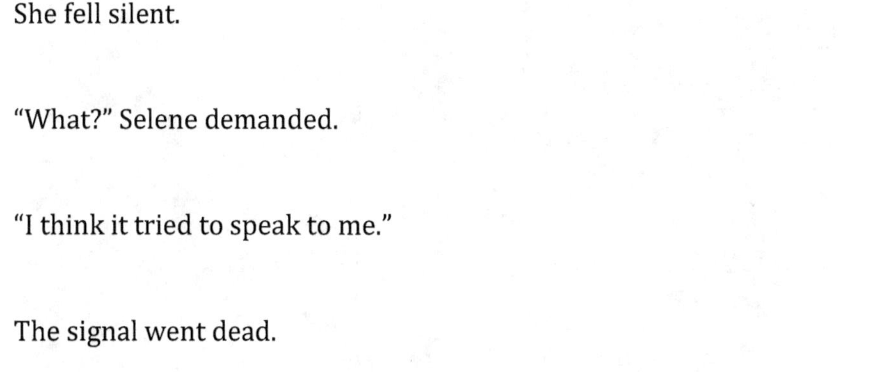

She fell silent.

"What?" Selene demanded.

"I think it tried to speak to me."

The signal went dead.

Selene stood in the quiet of the lab, the drawing still throbbing faintly on the screen.

She murmured, more to the room than to herself. "Ansel... who are you becoming?"

§

Chapter 3: Static Frequencies

¶

Part 1: The Buzz Beneath Silence

It had begun as a sigh—the faintest vibration at the very limits of audibility.

A slight pressure behind Selene's ears, as though the air itself were leaning in. It was not a headache, not the deep shudder of traffic below. It was simply the city's dull murmur, attenuated through the ceiling over the street.

Selene blinked away from the console's phosphor screens just as Ansel entered the room. He never walked through doors, drifted like the gentlest of rains on glass, mind unmoored. Barefoot, he glided over the glossy floorboards, each footfall a nearly silent susurration.

Her hand went to the matte curve of her bioaudio implant, caressing the seam between cold titanium and skin. She had tuned it only months ago, sensitive enough to hear the beat of a fly's wings across several floors.

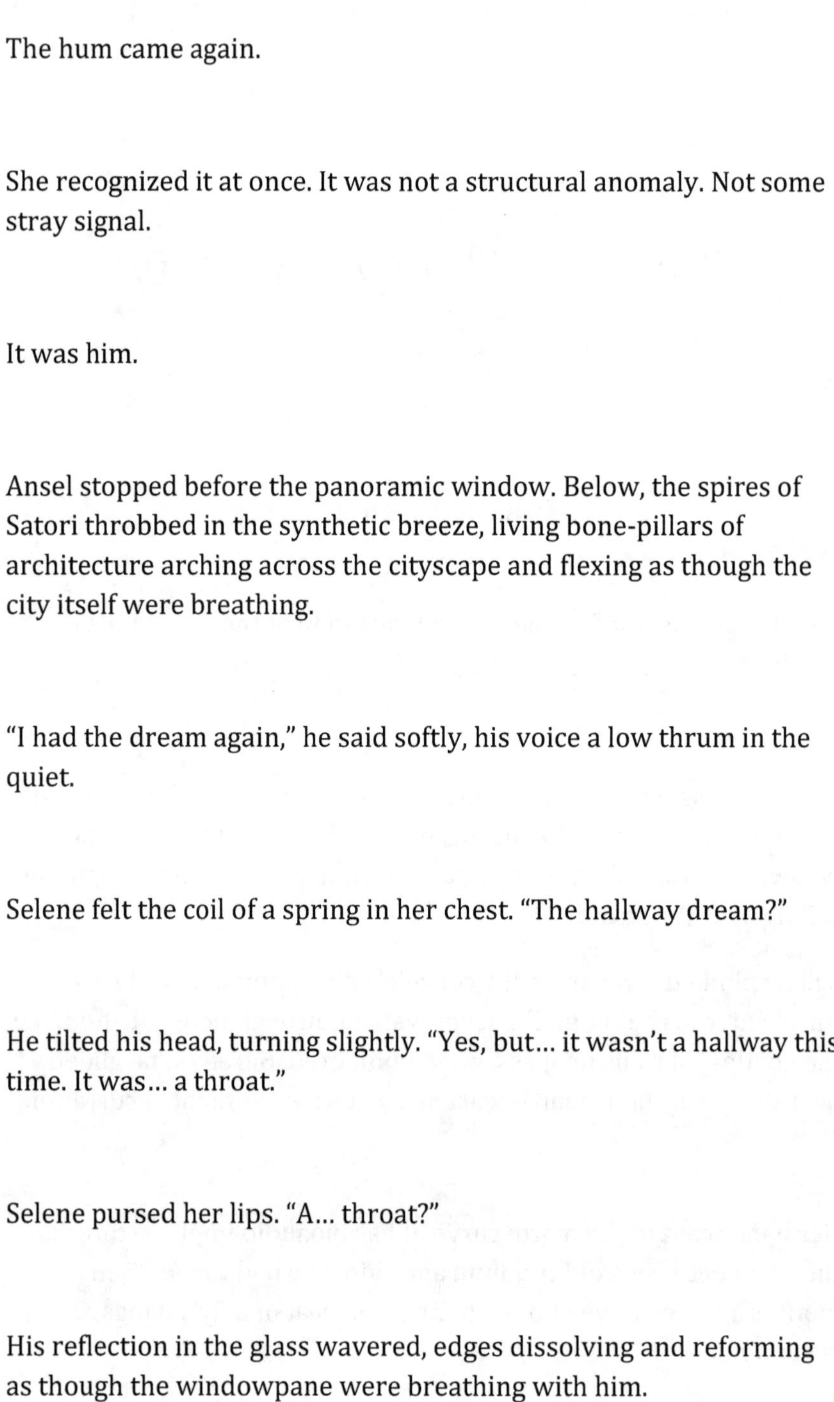

The hum came again.

She recognized it at once. It was not a structural anomaly. Not some stray signal.

It was him.

Ansel stopped before the panoramic window. Below, the spires of Satori throbbed in the synthetic breeze, living bone-pillars of architecture arching across the cityscape and flexing as though the city itself were breathing.

“I had the dream again,” he said softly, his voice a low thrum in the quiet.

Selene felt the coil of a spring in her chest. “The hallway dream?”

He tilted his head, turning slightly. “Yes, but… it wasn’t a hallway this time. It was… a throat.”

Selene pursed her lips. “A… throat?”

His reflection in the glass wavered, edges dissolving and reforming as though the windowpane were breathing with him.

“I could feel the walls pulsing,” he continued, tone remote. “Not stone, not metal, but muscle. It was alive—inhaling, blood coursing.”

Instinctively, Selene tapped one of the console’s crystalline nodes. The indicator glowed green. She initiated a diagnostic overlay in her audio band—automatic sweeps to detect the presence of foreign signals.

On the holo-screen, the data scrolled:

EXT VLF DETECTED: 6.3Hz

LOC: LOCALIZED

MODULATION: BIOLOGICAL

Selene’s heart stuttered. She ran a reverse-spectrum trace, the numbers reversing. The signal signature crystallized.

It wasn’t noise.

It was a heartbeat.

Three rapid taps. Two elongated pulses. A pregnant silence. Repeat.

The room swam. Selene grasped the edge of the console to steady herself. "Ansel… where did you hear that heartbeat?"

Slowly, as though emerging from another world, he rotated his head to face her. "I was never taught. It has always been whispered in the membrane of all things. I only recently began to hear."

Selene stepped closer. "Heard what?"

He raised his chin, eyes far away and primordially placid. "The underneath."

Step by step, she closed the distance between them. The heartbeat grew clearer—it was not anger, but presence. She could not hold focus as she neared him. The world melted at the edges.

"Okay," she said. Her voice was weak. "You have to sleep now."

His mouth curved, a half-smile—no childish smirk, but something deeper, slow, older than old. As he passed, the pulse fell away, as though a wire had been severed. Silence bloomed in the room—too vast, too loud to bear.

Selene sat at the console, watching the looping waveform scroll across the holo-screen. In the corner of the screen, the file name pulsed white:

Signal ID: Echo-Origin-One

¶

Part 2: The Hall of Sleepers

The med-center's facade was an obelisk of exotic flowers and brass, a glass-walled botanical garden without plants. It had been a plant conservatory, long since abandoned, then repurposed. Faux-petals and bioluminescent tendrils glowed at unnatural frequencies, undulating against cracked glass. Without training, it would take hours to spot the details only a geneticist would notice: the government's fingerprints.

Selene stepped through the outer security field, waving her hand for the receptionist's unspoken nod. Her clearance band pulsed a low amber on her wrist. The walls beyond the lobby flickered a low coral—another anxiety-neutralizing measure, designed to ease the mind. The air tasted of oxygenated lavender and menthol, with sharp bursts of citrus from vents along the walls. Selene had seen medical centers like this one, but never one so carefully curated.

"Dr. Miro." A voice, low and melodic, descended the hall.

Dr. Reva Taran opened the door to the adjacent room, a lab coat draped over her slumped shoulders. She was in charge of Dawn Phase Variance Observation—the euphemism for the children whose bodies and minds matured at unnatural rates—and there was something of the watchful mother in the way she regarded Selene. Her eyes were soft at first glance, but they flickered constantly outward, measuring and memorizing every detail.

"I wasn't sure you'd come." She took Selene's hand, cool and professional, but she was begging as much as instructing.

"I wasn't sure I should." Selene's fingers curled around Taran's, registering the slight tremor. Terror or something more complex, Selene couldn't say.

There were several frosted-glass rooms down the hall. Caretakers hunched silently in each. A humming machine buzzed a low, broken song from one. A woman without sound wept in another. In the third, a figure rocked back and forth, thumbing at a photo with the child's face warped by static, pixelated like a projection unwinding.

"They're not aggressive." Dr. Taran gestured toward the rooms. "The variance isn't explosive or dangerous. Their change is slow and insidious. You'll notice a stuttering in their vocabulary. Breaks in their circadian rhythm. Shifting favorites. Books, food, music, people. Then they start to lose things. Lose memory, like a file being deleted. The people who love them, at first, then sometimes they lose themselves." She paused. "The written record skips. Starts to get incoherent, like you're revising a narrative while you're in the middle of reading it."

"Is it spontaneous?" Selene asked. The hall echoed with its low luminosity.

"Always induced. Something at the right frequency. A catalyst to set off the chain reaction."

The two stopped in front of a blast door. Dr. Taran punched in a code, and the door slid open with a hiss.

The silence hit like a wall when they entered. The anteroom felt enormous, the sterility humid and thick, infused with a slight warmth, as if the space exhaled with relief when it closed behind them.

At its center, seven children lay in custom chairs. Their knees and elbows were cradled by sinewy fibers that wrapped and tightened, fabric coming to life. The children's faces were placid, eyelids long beneath fluttering lashes. A faint haze of moving light hovered around their heads—woven fields of adaptive crystal filament, dimming the outside noise and light. Their skin took on a luminescent hue. The blankets and pillows around them emitted a similar, lesser buzz. The entire room vibrated as if strummed by some distant force.

Selene advanced through the chamber, electric with awareness. She felt, more than heard, a low-frequency thumping in her chest and gut. A pulse of vibration that was almost subsonic, vibrating her skin. The edges of her vision flickered, like the world itself was stretching and compressing in front of her.

"This containment field isolates their resonance, keeps it from projecting beyond this room." Dr. Taran's voice was hushed with awe. “But the neural remapping—the rewriting of the ‘I’—begins hours after they’re exposed. And if the resonance they’re exposed to is a constant…” Her voice caught in her throat. “If they hear that thing again, the child you knew is gone.”

“They disappear?” Selene asked.

Dr. Taran’s mouth set firm. “They lose language. They lose emotion between them. The ‘I’ fragments.”

Selene stepped closer to the children. Their faces were soft, warm, and honey-lit by the shifting fields around them.

“And they dream?”

Instead of answering, she pressed a small decoder into Selene’s palm.

S-9’s harmonic layer.

The buds were cool in Selene’s ears. Nothing at first. Then—

A hum emerged from somewhere deep beneath her sternum. Not music. Not language. Ancient.

A series of voices braided together, woven with a meaning not needing words. One strand trembled tighter than the rest, vibrating with the clarity of recognition:

“We were never separate.”

Selene plucked the buds from her ears. Her heart pounded in her throat. “When do they wake up?”

Dr. Taran’s eyes never left the children. “They are not sleeping. They are waiting.”

¶

Part 3: Virel-Adran’s First Visit

Selene’s hand pressed against the haptic window of the observation room, looking out at the Akari Learning Sphere. The ring-shaped structure opened on one side, ascending and floating with a gentle shifting of weightless platforms in response to the occupants who moved around in the empathy field of anti-gravity. Cedar and salt hung in the air.

“There will be no visitors today,” the Dawn attendant told her at the door.

She peered at the holopane and saw her son. He sat alone at the center of a small circle, folded his hands in his lap, and did nothing. A visualization of the recorded feed overlaid the view with emotional mapping and intention heat maps. Memories encoded in data.

The air rippled. A man materialized in a shimmer of light.

Virel-Adran didn't walk so much as appear, called by the room. Robes of dusk and rain shifted as he moved across the floor to the small cluster of platforms where the boy sat. She had not seen him in ten years.

The communication was only in resonance lines, and what language shared was unclear.

Virel-Adran sat opposite Ansel, and there was silence. The two of them exchanged nothing that Selene could see. The air pressure shifted around them. Platform screens turned dark blue, indigo. Plants along the wall edges uncoiled, listening.

The frequency line jittered.

Selene leaned in.

She leaned close until a pinprick of data was all she could make out against the glowing arcs and sensors in the room. Then she saw it, and she leaned in closer still.

Then it happened. Something she could not understand. The harmonics reversed. The frequency line blinked as energy ricocheted between the two of them, creating a closed-loop feedback matrix. A pristine communication. Something Selene's entire research career told her that could not be, according to the principles of Virelian Linguistic Theory.

Ansel sat up, eyes wide with a dawning awareness beyond his years.

Virel-Adran set one palm flat against the floor. After a moment, Ansel copied him, palms flat against the ground, fingers twitching and reaching only inches apart.

"What are you doing to him?" Selene whispered against the pane.

Virel-Adran pressed his lips together in nonhuman articulations of a form of communication Selene had long thought dead. Her translation app spat back:

LANGUAGE UNRECOGNIZED

SOURCE ERROR: NON-TEMPORAL PHONETICS

Ansel's eyes fluttered shut, and a deep peacefulness crossed his features.

The ambient lights in the room dimmed as if the entire space strained to listen. The plants on the periphery of the room curled inwards, photosensors pricked up, then everything reset to its base setting.

The Virelian rose with the elegance that was common to his species, bowed his head in respect to Ansel, and left without another word.

Selene exhaled a breath she didn't realize she was holding, fingernails white on the observation console.

The door behind her clicked with a digital chime.

"You're contaminating my research subject," she began, turning on her heel, voice clipped with restrained offense.

"Dr. Miro." Virel-Adran's voice gave him away; it still bore the diplomatic distance of a decade between them. "Your work is, as always, admirable."

"You have no business approaching my son without permission. I don't care if you're family." She straightened her back and met his sea-glass eyes.

His mouth curled at the corner of his lip. "I did not choose this. The resonance led me to him."

“Can we stick to science and leave the mysticism out?” She tapped at her tablet. “What did you tell him?”

“Only what was already rising in him.”

“That is not an answer.” She squinted at him. She was a scientist, and she wanted the truth.

Virel-Adran turned to the observation chamber, pressing himself against the viewing glass that showed the emptiness of the room where Ansel had sat. The alien’s throat bobbed a short distance from his eyes. “Your son is awakening ancestral memory engrams. The latent neurological pathways are opening.”

“In English, Adran.”

He turned to her, eyes dark. “Selene, the future we thought we were building has already arrived.”

¶

Part 4: Harmonic Memory Transfer

Selene sat in the lab's blackness, helmet buckled tight, senses sealed. She faced the console, and the filtered tone—harvested from Ansel's dreams—was about to play. Her heart was pounding.

Playback: Echo-Origin-One. Duration: 38 seconds.

"Ready." She whispered.

The sound was a low thrum. It pulsed up her spine. She swallowed hard, panic squeezing her throat. In the instant before her lids flew back and images flooded in, she had a moment of pure, exquisite gold.

A blood-red sky, a cracked and blackened stone floor. Two moons, rising slowly against the far wall—one chalk-white, the other an empty black hole. Heat. Silence. And then, a single word, a word she felt in her marrow instead of hearing with her ears:

"Again."

The earth opened up beneath her, and Selene felt herself unravel—identity ripped from her core, only to be born again. It was a deep, primeval rush, with no pain to speak of—only sensation. Shrieking, she ripped off the helmet and slumped to the floor. Choking bile rose in her throat as her lungs struggled as though they'd only just broken water. The whole world shook, and her vision was a kaleidoscope of white spots.

Thirty-eight seconds. The loop had ended. Someone else's death had been delivered. Selene crawled to the console, cut the feed, and shrouded the file with six layers of encryption. But deep in her bones, she knew that she had changed, not just a witness but an agent. She had been there.

¶

Part 5: The Unseen Choir

The walk home had felt untethered tonight. Selene clung to the shadowed backstreets of New Satori's western flank, where the neon crowds had thinned to deserted avenues and the roar of her blood drummed in her temples. The memory transfer still pulsed against her skin—a tremor she could not yet identify.

Glass towers crowned the alleys above in monuments of light. A brackish wind twisted around the streets, copper scents and sugared cherry blossom bark. Genetically modified Virelian songbirds crooned programmed refrains from above, low harmonics to clear the mind.

It did not help.

She passed halfway through an arched plaza when she saw them. Seven Dawn teenagers, each probably no older than sixteen. Pale capes pooled on their shoulders. Bioluminescent hair threads pulsed with the cadence of their breath.

Faces blank, bodies rigid.

They said nothing.

They did nothing.

They simply stood.

Silent.

Statuesque.

The palm of one boy cupped the air. The parted lips of one girl whispered in mute supplication.

Selene stilled beneath the arch; the air thickened around her.

She tried to move forward. Her legs would not obey. A soft but urgent hum filled her ears. Her bio-audio wrist band began to vibrate against her skin in steady pulses.

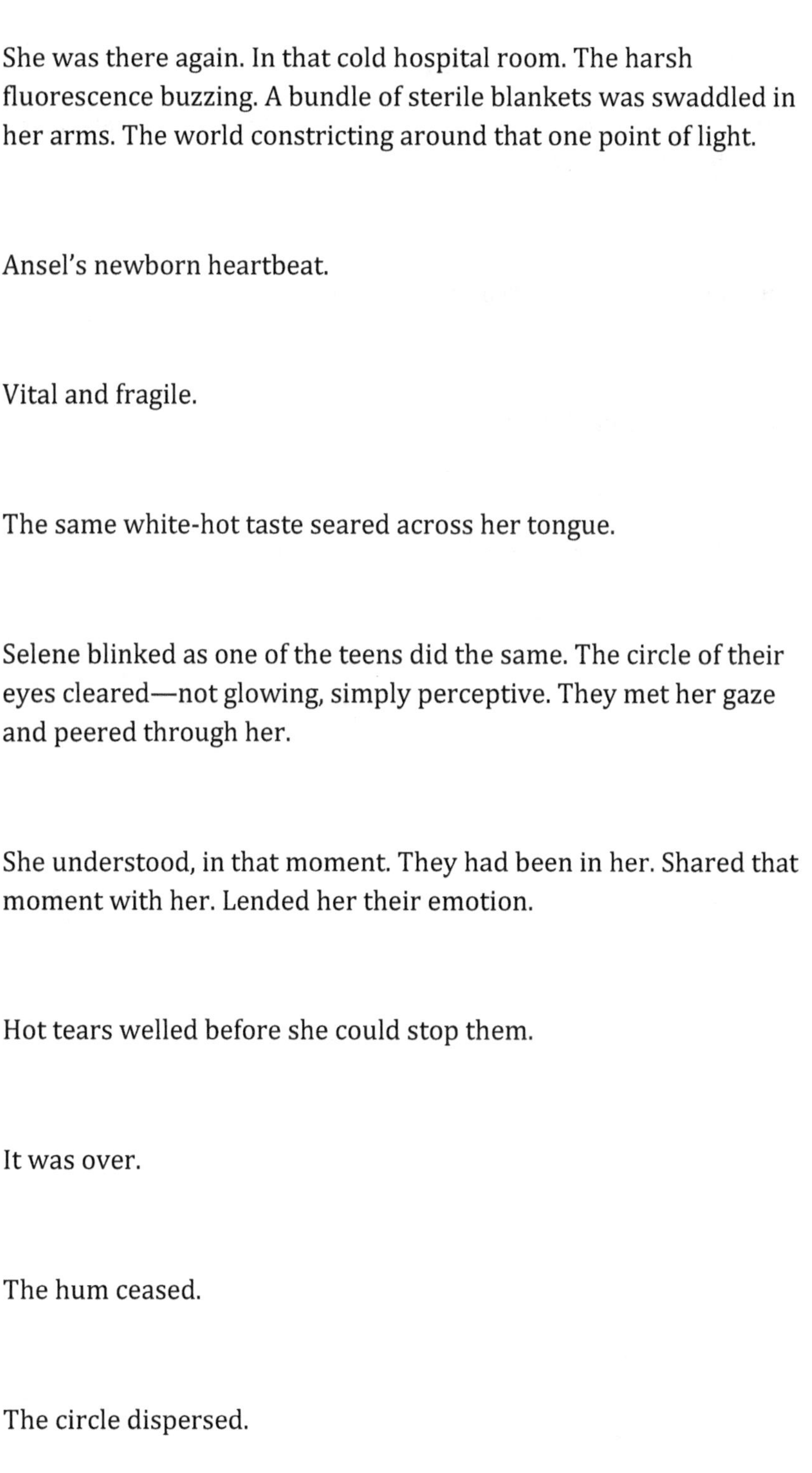

She was there again. In that cold hospital room. The harsh fluorescence buzzing. A bundle of sterile blankets was swaddled in her arms. The world constricting around that one point of light.

Ansel's newborn heartbeat.

Vital and fragile.

The same white-hot taste seared across her tongue.

Selene blinked as one of the teens did the same. The circle of their eyes cleared—not glowing, simply perceptive. They met her gaze and peered through her.

She understood, in that moment. They had been in her. Shared that moment with her. Lended her their emotion.

Hot tears welled before she could stop them.

It was over.

The hum ceased.

The circle dispersed.

The teens scuttled away, giggling and talking amongst themselves as if nothing had occurred.

Selene stayed under the archway, shaking, eyes bleared.

They had not meant to hurt her.

They had simply wanted her to feel. To remember.

§

Chapter 4: Echo Market

¶

Part 1: The Coral Steps

The sky was shrouded in thin white fog. Below the New Satori, the Echo Market unfurled into the ribbed hull of the ancient ship Athenra. Colorful coraline growths clung to its fossilized bones.

Selene perched on the lip and looked down at the terraces etched into the open-air bazaar. Coral-stone steps twinkled in the twilight beneath her boots—warm, almost alive.

The first time she'd come to Echo Market, Ansel was three and had clung to her leg, afraid of every shadowed alcove and entranced by the singing stairs. Now he'd walk those terraces alone—fearless, and without her.

Selene dropped down into the market. Stalls of Virelian bio-jewelry, empathic textiles, polished mind-seed husks, and softly luminescent memory stones filled the terraces. Hybrid crowds—humans, Dawns, Virelians—threaded through in practiced synchronicity. Polite. Calm.

But the silence was too complete. Too expectant. Like a stadium, just before the drop.

A cluster of whisper-pods buzzed nearby—micro-organic advertisements that murmured straight into thoughts. Selene snapped her wrist and sent a burst of neural static through her implant. They fell silent.

At the edge of the spiral, in a crevice beneath a living coral monolith, a man hunched over a nest of neural husks and old analog tech. He raised his head, heavy-lidded eyes brightening in a crooked grin.

"You still walk like you're afraid someone will see you." He continued. "Which means you're still interesting."

"Hello, Daen." Selene lowered her hood.

Daen Hurl—formally a neuroscientist, currently a black-market trader in brain scraps and illegal memory loops—gestured at a small iron case on the ground between them. "Your message said you had something."

Selene arched an eyebrow.

He thumbed a small locked iron case next to him. "It's not broadcasting. Doesn't have to."

Selene said nothing, eyeing the case.

Daen's grin faded. "Started pulsing yesterday. Right after you opened your kid's dream file." He thumbed the case.

"Sync signal. Exact frequency."

"Organic material doesn't sync with lab equipment." Selene's instinct to question rose in her like an old reflex.

Memory-bud. Daen's eyes shone with the pride of a collector. "Salvaged it from an abandoned nest. Grew like a parasite on the walls." He chuckled, dark pride in his voice. "Outer Quarters."

Selene's hand twitched over the case. She could feel it, could sense it somehow from beneath the cold iron surface. An organic pattern. A dim pulse that was not a heartbeat, not a signal, but something...waiting.

"What the hell am I looking at?" Her voice dropped a half octave by instinct.

Daen chuckled and leaned back in the warm shadows of the stairwell. "A Dream without a dreamer."

¶

Part 2: The Trader of Forgotten Names

Selene had come from Daen's stall, the iron case heavy and darkly shining in her hands. The spiral wound back upon itself in ever-decreasing loops, a series of narrow walkways roofed with strips of dyed silk that fluttered like imprisoned wings and hung above streetlamps that were hollow glass scent-globes. As she passed, the globes popped softly. Some burst with tart citrus, others with the smell of brine-saturated air or the hot dust of old paper.

Here was where the Memory Traders came to trade.

Beneath a slanting awning of solar chitin (translucent panels held together by giant insect wings woven together in a shimmering network), an old woman sat cross-legged on a rough woven mat. Spread out before her on the ground were a circle of smooth stones, chilled and slate-gray, and a pile of slim metal rings—brass, copper, silver, all stamped with a single name. Some were etched into crystals, others were burned into thin sheets of folded bark, but all the letters were handwritten and as fine as spider silk.

No sign advertised what she did, no holo-interface blinked at her. Instead, chalked in pale white letters on the crumbly stone wall behind her was a simple sentence:

"What we choose to forget still remembers us."

Selene walked carefully. Lines had etched themselves deep into Mathe's face over the years, but her eyes, one warm brown and the other a whirring digital lens that scrolled invisible glyphs, were unmistakable.

"Mathe," Selene said quietly.

The woman did not look up. "Selene Miro," she said dryly. "I didn't need to wait long for you. You're practically crackling."

Selene sat down on her heels. "Are you still harvesting?"

Mathe raised her eyes to meet Selene's. "I don't harvest. I collect. These names—these were Dawns who stepped away from their former lives. Some give their name, some won't speak at all."

Selene lifted a thin brass ring, etched with the name "Liora," and turned it in her hands. "Are they all… really gone?"

"They're not dead," Mathe said, "but they're done."

Slowly, Selene placed the ring back on the ground. "I didn't bring you here to have a tour."

Mathe reached behind her and took down a small package swathed in a dull blue cloth. She handed it over into Selene's waiting hands. "It was delivered four days ago. No—four days before, I think. I mean, it found me. I wasn't planning on letting it go."

Selene unwrapped the cloth. Inside, resting on a bed of moss was a memory-seed the size of a marble, its surface gnarled and pitted like volcanic rock. Fine glowing filaments curled around the central core of the seed. They pulsed soft green as soon as it was unwrapped.

Selene flinched. Though she hadn't touched it, it knew her presence. It was synchronizing, humming.

Mathe regarded her. "It will only respond to those who are resonance-linked. Twelve have come before you. Not one has survived. But you are different, Selene—"

Selene swallowed. "What is inside of it?"

"A pre-resonance dream," Mathe said, her voice a whisper. "Encoded before the Dawns. Before any kind of contact."

"That's not possible," Selene whispered.

Mathe tilted her head. "It is not."

Selene held her hand a fraction of an inch above the seed. It throbbed beneath her fingers—slow, and insistent, like a heartbeat but under that something else, a flicker of recognition.

She withdrew her hand after a moment, long and silent. "I'm not ready."

"Then it is not time." Mathe wrapped the seed in its blue shroud once more.

Selene turned back to walk away, but Mathe's quiet voice followed her into the narrow walkway:

"When the name you bear is no longer your own, do not grieve it. That is how stars die—and how they are reborn."

¶

Part 3: Protest at the Fountain

The usual background buzz of the plaza was different today. Not louder, just sharper. She moved from the tight alleyways into the plaza's center, the smell of hot metal and cinnamon rolls mingling with dusty echoes of that blasted, omnipresent Heartwell fountain. Normally, she found comfort in its steady thrumming, the dull roar of old Virelian engineering, but today its rhythm held the tension of impending rain.

Voices had been washing over her since she first stepped outside. A man atop a crate near the fountain waved his arms, his rugged Sovereign Continuum jacket flapping against his frame. He was holding a handheld amp and was shouting in the middle of the city's marketplace.

"This is the future they sold us—a false peace built on the theft of our birthright!" The man's voice boomed across the plaza, vibrating in Selene's chest. Anger hummed in the crowd around her, hot and thick in the lungs of the protesters. Fervor ran in ragged waves.

Selene found herself on the edge of the crowd, heart pounding. She used to understand his message—she almost believed in the integrity of pure heritage. But she also remembered the prickling skepticism that came when the protest leader shouted about parents and their stolen children's voices. Could you erase the fissures in culture without also cutting the threads of individuality? Did he see what she saw? The taste of iron returned to Selene's mouth.

He jabbed a finger at a holo-projected image of a child. "Six years old. The last words she said to her father? Goodbye. She dissolved herself into someone else's mind—and left him crying in the gardens of a city he'd never seen!" A low, animalistic roar moved through the crowd—a mixture of cheer and disgust.

Selene glanced inward, palms twitching. She sympathized with the refugees. With those whose minds had been scrambled by empathy. But she also feared the erasure of self, of being half-herself in a shared pool. Selene's lungs ached as each raised fist and shouted chant pulled another noose tight around her throat.

And then she saw the child. Selene's breath caught in her chest at the figure half-obscured by a vendor's cart at the base of the fountain. An eight-year-old Dawn girl, with hair braided into comet tails. The child's eyes were wide and unblinking as she watched the scene before her.

Selene could not say what it was about the child's stillness in the face of all this chaos that rang like a gong through her mind. She felt it all the same, as if someone had punched the air out of her lungs, forcing her to take a slow and calming breath. All that mattered in that breath was the protest leader's shouting voice, the persistent thrum of the fountain, and the presence of the girl in the plaza with her.

In that moment, the crowd around Selene blurred and faded into noisy irrelevance. Her body moved before her mind could process the motion. She was rushing forward, as if into a fight she could not hope to win, before she even understood what she was doing.

She found herself at the fountain's edge, knees drawn up to her chest, hands clutching the hem of her tunic.

She didn't know when the Dawn girl started humming. Barely audible above the continuous thrum of the plaza, she heard the vibration first against her skin, then as a sound: a memory of a lullaby her grandmother had sung when she was a child, a spark of electricity running through her brain.

The sound ebbed through her chest—not intrusive but warm and beckoning, like heat from a fire. It was something she had known but did not know until that moment. Something she had been waiting for but had never consciously acknowledged.

The crowd around the fountain stilled in ripples outward from the source of the sound.

Wait, what is—? The protest leader's amplifier clattered from his hands and splintered on the crate beneath him.

A woman near Selene laughed, a sound of pure joy. Next to her, a gray-haired man cupped his hands around his eyes. Two strangers across the plaza grabbed each other's hands.

The girl continued to hum. The sound spiraled out from the child and interwove with the fountain's vibration until sound and water became one, and the plaza held its breath.

The protest leader slumped to his knees, tears streaming across the dust of his face. "My mother," he said, through white knuckles, "in the garden, with the blue flowers. I'd forgotten..."

The plaza did not move until the humming had ended. The crowd around the fountain stood in shared intimacy, too close to one another for anyone to utter a sound.

Selene pushed past the crowd, but several Virelian peacekeepers with silver-trimmed robes were already there to take the girl from the plaza. She glanced back once at the child as she was led away. Her face was a tangle of confusion and alarm.

No one was arrested. No one was charged. The plaza did not disperse.

Selene stayed at the plaza's edge for a long time, staring. The research she had been conducting these last months now burned bright and clear in her head. This had not been some secret Dawn agenda—this was not tactical telepathy, emotional manipulation, or crowd control. This was evolution.

¶

Part 4: The Fear of Peace

The plaza felt... thin. It was not quiet, not exactly: strands of sound clung in the air like cobwebs. The Heartwell Fountain's insistent cyclical hum, the soft susurrus of collapsing bodies, the ghost of a gasp that trailed into nothing. But there was a new silence where there had been screams and fighting, the drumming of many feet stamping out in unison.

Selene leaned against a vine-wrapped column, her heart still drumming from the tide of something she could not quite place. It was not fear. It was not wonder. It was something colder. She allowed herself to watch.

The wild-eyed man who had burst from the crate only moments before now knelt cross-legged at the plaza's center, hands pressed to his face. Two people knelt at his sides, arms pulling him against them and holding in his sobbing breaths. "I forgot her hands… the way they smelled after she peeled onions," he choked out. "I forgot…" His voice shattered the quiet each time.

Nearby, a woman let out a small, laughing sigh through tears. "I don't know why I'm crying," she said, mostly to herself. "It's like someone just told me they forgave me." She shrugged and slumped. A figure in robes of pale blue and green hovered above them all. A Virelian peacekeeper, but they moved with no authority. They seemed not to govern broken men and women so much as shepherd them. They approached the Dawn girl, trembling at their feet. The child wore a pair of wide, hollow eyes and a deer caught in headlights expression. The peacekeeper knelt, reached out a hand to brush the girl's shoulder. "I just got scared," the girl whispered. The peacekeeper gave a single nod. "You were heard."

Wave after wave of release washed over the crowd. An uncomfortable calm settled over every face: a peace not of their choosing, given without consent. They did not fight it. Some even smiled.

Selene tore her gaze away, hand tightening on the case Daen had given her. If an unmodulated shout of emotion could quiet an entire plaza, what would a well-harmonized choir do?

¶

Part 5: Echoes Without Consent

The playback looped over and over in Selene's lab, bathing her weary face in an unearthly blue.

She had been analyzing it for sixteen hours now. Frame by frame, spectrum by spectrum. Sound. Movement. Biological field activity. Resonance patterning. Her fingers shook slightly as she worked the holographic playback controls. They always did when she was close to something.

"Play the crowd response again for me," she mumbled, her voice rough from lack of use.

Spread out in the analysis window in front of her: all of them, everyone in that plaza square, all of them having reacted not to the Dawn child's humming but to something invisible—a field that had quietly reconfigured their emotions, a bug patch for the soul.

She was seeing it again now.

Frame 973. Timecode 16:04:23. The first frame in which the child hummed.

Zooming in on the child's face: wide eyes. Pale complexion. Shaking hands. Dilated pupils.

"She was not singing," Selene said quietly. "She was scared."

The field had triggered itself.

Selene sagged back in her chair with a protest from the worn springs. Her hand went to her sternum, the place where her heart was pounding in her ribs. It had been there. The evidence was there. The frequency spike that had begun all this had not been generated by any kind of conscious neural command. It had been a defensive biocognitive spasm, a self-protection empathy loop. The Dawn girl had been terrified, and her emotions had pushed their way into everyone else.

This was not a learned behavior. This was evolution.

There was a ping from the console that made Selene jump. TESS, her onboard AI interface, pulsed online with its characteristic cyan flicker. "Do you wish to record a social deviance filing with the City Consensus Board?"

Selene's throat constricted.

"Would you like to save the analysis review?" TESS prompted again.

She said nothing. For a long moment, she did not move. This was not about reporting something anymore. This was a choice she had been putting off for months.

The Dawns were dangerous, not because they wanted to be. The Dawns were dangerous because they didn't have to choose to be. Simply by being, they were already there. And the resonance they made, the beautiful singularity of peace—none of it was a choice.

It would overwrite humanity.

Not by force.

But by proximity.

Selene pushed herself to her feet, knees stiff from hours of sitting. She found her eyes drawn to the case next to her console, the locked case where the memory-seed Daen had given her was stored. It was currently humming softly to itself, the glow pulses synced now to the beat of her heart.

She took a deep breath. For a long moment, Selene allowed herself to be honest. To say the truth that had been gestating in her mind for weeks.

"They won't even have to take the world."

Selene's eyes drifted down the hallway to the door with her son's name on it.

"We'll give it to them."

§

Chapter 5: The Weeping Sleep

¶ Part 1: The Crying Without Cause

The house was quiet, but not empty.

Selene awoke before her neural alarm sounded—not a chime, just that old familiar weight in her chest. She sat up and took in the hallway. Ansel's door was cracked, the biolattice frame faintly throbbing, as if beckoning her in.

She tiptoed across the slick floor and into his darkened room, biothread vines overhead throwing muted light across the floor. Ansel sat on his bed's edge, shoulders hunched, hands fisted in the blanket at his knees. He did not look at her.

"Mom..." He mumbled, voice low and pinched.

Selene crouched next to him. "You were dreaming."

He shook his head. "I was... in-between." He inhaled sharply. "Like a bridge. You don't exist at either end. And below me... it was crying.

But not mine." He clenched his jaw, as if he had to hold back words to keep them from shattering him.

Selene placed a hand on his arm. He flinched but did not retract. "Whose is it?"

His eyes closed, he thought of the day his squad had gone quiet in the desert, the reverberation he could never outrun.

"I don't know."

He exhaled shakily and lay back against the pillows, dragging the blankets up to his chin. His eyes were on the ceiling.

"Stay with me?" Selene murmured.

He shook his head. "Not when it comes."

Selene stood and hesitated, then took her place in the doorway—unyielding as a sentinel—observing him, struggling against a darkness he could not name.

¶

Part 2: Data from the Broken Night

Selene had commandeered the old neuro-mapping rig in the lab by morning. She'd only used it once—years ago, on the Dawn field teams, when sleep divergence first began to infiltrate the crew. Even then, it had felt invasive: the tech didn't just monitor REM, it traced every spark of conscious awareness, every incomplete memory. It was banned.

She hadn't slept in days. Instead, she'd fiddled, tinkered, recalibrated, and remapped.

By late afternoon, the machine thrummed to readiness. Selene claimed it was for "observation." Ansel didn't object. He simply shrugged and said, "I won't argue with it any longer. Maybe it's time you watched, too."

That night, Selene watched from behind the reinforced observation panel. Ansel lay beneath a soft lattice of neural tendrils, the monitor nodes twinkling against the filaments woven into the living wall of the room.

His eyes closed. The machine whirred to life. First, the familiar alpha, theta, and delta patterns she could recognize in her sleep. Then the hitch in his breathing—and a blip on the resonance array. Selene leaned in.

On the screen, an impossible spiral unfurled. Not the smooth ripples of a brainwave but a tight coil, curling inward and taut as a coiled spring. Over and over it looped, each tendril spiraling down.

The console blinked its diagnosis: "**Δ-Spiral/Res Pattern Detected — Class: Recursive Bioharmonic.**"

Then the spiral splintered, and the rig chirped a warning. "**DATA PULSE DETECTED. NON-RANDOM. ENCRYPTED SEQUENCE.**"

Selene hesitated over the controls. Her fingers hovered. She froze and captured the sequence, running it through the clean-room filter. Nothing: no synthetic residues, no cross-contamination. This wasn't noise—it was language.

One fragment in the sequence stood out: a tiny burst like a punctuation mark. She highlighted it and slowed the playback. On the screen, three nested rings pulsed in symmetrical cadence.

She felt them—everywhere, not just in her headphones but in the hollow of her chest, under her skin, down to her teeth, like the ghost of a forgotten memory.

The console pinged. "**Signal match: 62.4% overlap with Class-3 Virelian ancestral resonance.**"

That couldn't be. Ansel had never encountered Class-3 markers—those were found in pre-Contact ruins, long predating the earliest records of Virelian history.

Selene stared in silence. The spiral unfurled again, more slowly this time, deliberate. Buried in the coils were nine hard spikes, equally spaced.

Not Morse code. Something older. Something...counting down.

¶

Part 3: The Map That Feels

Selene's fingers hovered above the resonance translator.

Ghostly in the black of the console screen, she saw her own face.

It was her design, made long ago with the hopes of translating Dawn vocalizations into something legible. Something patterned like recognizable emotions. As of yet, all it had been able to find in recordings were basic responses. Happy, hungry, impatient. Human. Basic.

But Ansel's dream spiral didn't fit the pattern. It was not a vocalization. It wasn't even quite linguistic. But it was strong. Purposeful. Not just noise.

She plugged the waveform into the translator.

The reaction was immediate. The screen did not display the data; it translated. Simple emotional markers bled out across the decoding gel and into the pattern. Not complex, but too deep to easily categorize. There was a foundation to it: a yearning. A presence. Then a spark of recognition.

The translator started to stutter. Emotional markers replayed in bursts that first seemed like a breakdown, but Selene saw what it was coalescing into. Not random—patterned.

And then it clicked.

Pattern did not resolve to screen as language, but as understanding:

“We remember your silence.”

The translator looped the phrase, a replay that shifted emotional context each time it repeated. Shame. Depth. Guilt. Like layers of sediment.

“Who are ‘we’?” Selene asked. Her voice was cold where a knot in her throat should have been.

"We remember your silence." the translator replied. It was almost a whisper.

Selene leaned back in her chair, thinking. This wasn't Ansel. This wasn't a message to her.

This was something that reminded her.

¶

Part 4: Writing on the Wall

The house hummed around her. A vibrating buzz echoed in her chest. Selene's eyes shot open. Curfew had tripped the bio-architect. A soft static buzz underlined the unbidden movement.

She swung her legs off the bed. "Where is he?"

TESS's soothing voice responded: **"Ansel is in the atrium. Dreamstate undisturbed. Vital signs stable."**

He was sleepwalking again.

Selene fumbled with her robe and staggered down the hall. Walls throbbed awake with wake-light keeping time with her hammering pulse. Humid air clung to her when she finally opened the atrium door.

Ansel stood shirtless before a living wall. One hand flat against the surface, fingers curving over biostructure. Sharp glyphs fanned out from his touch; intertwining arcs, calligraphy only he could read.

Panic clutched at Selene's chest. Every time he did this, she wondered if he was chasing something she could never understand.

Selene closed the distance between them. "Ansel."

He cocked his head in her direction; his eyes remained shut. "Yes?"

"Are you awake?"

He shook his head. "No."

"What...?"

"I'm remembering."

Selene watched his fingers brush two meters of carved syntax onto the wall, which ended up looking like scar tissue after he was done. When he finally crumpled, she caught him before his knees met the floor. His breathing evened, and he was gone.

Selene's hand flew to the nutrient-vine couch and yanked the heat-weave blanket over his shoulders. She lay him on the couch and searched for her spectrosonic recorder.

Back in the lab, she overlaid the wall's pattern on her Virel-Adran empathic spectrosonic reading. Curves of the glyphs matched—visual counterparts of resonance syllables meant to be heard, not seen or spoken.

Ansel hadn't carved them. He'd heard them—lost in dreams, and calling him back deeper than memory.

Selene realized with a gasp: These glyphs were more than wall code. They were the key to his mind—and to whatever secret he was running toward in sleep.

¶

Part 5: The Translation Fracture

Selene's breath froze. She did not dare blink. It had been nearly twenty-two hours since she'd last slept. The tubes above her head shone a bare amber to keep her from photoreflex migraines, but her hands did not hesitate. They were ice on the black, polished surface of the neural-composite screen, pads alive with wavering bioluminescent indicators.

The crystalline screen before her was bisected by a massive scan-density lattice. On the left, dozens upon dozens of tightly-scanned grids replicated the glyphs she'd imaged on Ansel's wall: tight whorls, pointed chevrons, tiny knots of string. On the right, the data blossomed: Dawnian neurallinguistic waveforms, Virelian articulation-resonance charts that twisted and fractured like mirages above a heatwave, and, incongruously, single glyph segments from petroglyphs carved into Neolithic Siberian permafrost and African desert stone.

No matter how one looked at it, none of these had any reason to know of the other. But in that moment...

The language translator program—a swarm of discreet cores throbbing through quantum-threaded parallelization—twitched and spooled out threads of possible cross-linkage. Three glyphs matched Dawn emotive vowels, the gentler, elliptical swell of bereavement and yearning. Five matched the cadence of Virelian ancestor-chants, long waves of somber pitch that resonated in her skull like old bells. And two—only two—seemed to match the faint whorls pressed into the engraved face of a funerary tablet entombed by glaciers for thousands of years.

A knot formed in her stomach. The program stuttered, trembled, then burst forth to completion. The translated statement inked itself across the screen in broken, brutish lines of text, primal and undeniable:

I was here when you left me. I waited. I became you.

Selene did not move. The stutter of her pulse synchronized with the text's flickering. It was not a threat. It was not a command. But it was unerasable. It was not inscribed with arrogant portent, but murmured from the depths of memory.

Left who? Her first thought, but she killed it, too. Left when? The second, and her chest closed in tightness—and she did not care.

Slowly, she did the only thing she could. She right-clicked, in sequence: she saved the native-translation file. Compressed it. Renamed it. Encrypted it with an old passphrase she'd last used the day she went offline to mourn her partner. She seared it onto a failsafe cold drive, its casing warming only in her fingerprint as she closed it, and nestled it inside the hollow base of a spare ceramic teacup—blue on the inside—on her shelf. She left no tracks, no records. No logs, no timestamps, no hint of any record. With care, she danced her gloved hands through the systems again, sifting all archival and tracking archives for stray crumbs of reference.

In the amber, she watched the plain wall behind her. It had been white, before she had marred it with the echo of a child's dream, voiced in a dead, impossible language. The phrase, like a pulse, fluttered in her head:

I became you.

Not “I replaced you.” Not “I killed you.” But “I became you.”

And more troubling than its meaning was the feeling that it raised in her. Fear. No. Something else.

Understanding.

§

Chapter 6: The Sound of Bone Changing

¶

Part 1: Group Session Gamma

The Gamma Chamber vibrated.

Ten Dawn children sat in a circle, hands together, forming a complete circuit of flesh and heartbeat. The living walls of the room pulsed in sympathy to adolescent neural patterns.

In the center, the Virelian instructor Searh-Adel remained perfectly still. Their translucent skin glowed with amber undertones as neuroconductive filaments floated from their sleeve cuffs.

"Initiate convergence," they intoned, their voice a low wash.

Ten eyelids snapped shut.

Bioharmonic filaments cascaded from the ceiling of the room to interlace with the hair of each child. Creating ghostly auras of light that hovered around their heads. They were not machines. They were listening.

Selene sat in the observation room with her fingers pressed together and her knuckles to her lips. Just monitoring. Nothing more.

Her eyes remained on Ansel, two to the left. Perfectly still.

But there, three places over—Rohen. His foot was jittering in an irregular pattern. Rhythmic but still not. Shallow breaths. His fingers were slowly and self-consciously contorting against his neighbors' palms.

Searh-Adel must have noticed as well. "The space between you is safe," they said, the closest thing to a placating tone that Searh-Adel's Virelian accent could muster. "The room is strong."

The floor vibrated, a low harmonic that resonated in her knee joints as the empathic convergence began. The first steps would be simple: feelings of happiness, acknowledgment, or inquiry—primary bonding harmonics.

Rohen jerked.

A third Dawn girl blinked. Nima, she recognized, Ansel's childhood friend. The pupil of her eye widened as her mind approached what was coming next.

Searh-Adel's filaments momentarily trembled but they continued.

The Gamma Chamber dropped three octaves below the range of human hearing. Selene felt it in her molars first. Then in the center of her sternum.

Rohen's body contorted, his spine bending in an unnatural arc. Head almost reaching his heels before he fell sideways and away from the circle of hands. His fingers loosened in a gasp.

The second wave cascaded along the bioskin walls. The sentient membrane of the Gamma Chamber compressed like a pair of lungs suffering from constriction.

Selene's knuckles turned white against the glass of the observation window.

Rohen reached for his chest and opened his mouth to scream, but no sound came out. A vibration began, from somewhere in his torso, inaudible to Selene but enough to cause the EEG monitors and other diagnostics in the room to flicker.

It made the sound of stalagmites under enormous pressure. The point right before fracturing.

All of the other Dawns jerked as one. Ansel's features contorted as tears streamed silently down his face. It wasn't fear—Selene had seen that look before on his face when his childhood pet died. Empathy, pure and raw.

"Keep him still, gently," Searh-Adel intoned, their movements that were once fluid and graceful now crisp, almost robotic.

Neural gel slithered over Rohen's skull. Two violent convulsions, then quiet.

The room was silent.

Hands unclasped. Children sighed.

Selene could hear her own heartbeat in the void. This was not a deviation. This was new. This was unrecorded.

"Disconnect," she said, her voice clear despite the shaking in her fingers. "Give me the full readout. Raw. No compression. No filters."

She already knew the diagnostics would find:

"That was not his voice."

¶

Changing Part 2: The Infrasound Spike

The MedTech bay was quiet. Biosilicate walls—Virelian composites that absorb trauma frequencies—buzzed slightly with contained tension. Monitors hummed, running data. The Dawn child was sedated on the table, two silent guards by their sides.

Selene stood next to the Chief Resonance Officer Yuri Tan—towering, exact, with gloved hands tracing patterns on the console. Yuri pulled up the newest audio capture: a single waveform, looping.

She replayed it. Then again. The shape never altered. No formants for speech. No inhalations. Only a slow, subsonic thrum.

"This isn't phonation," Yuri murmured. She flipped to volumetric scan, peeling away layers of flesh and muscle to find the skeleton. "See here—sternum."

On the hologram, the breastbone glowed, oscillating infinitesimally as if plucked by an invisible finger. Yuri overlaid the frequency data, which was a 14.1 hertz—deep, in the infrasound range.

"In Virelian fields, we've only observed this during profound sleep states and mourning practices," she went on, gaze not leaving the scan. "Never in living human tissue"

Selene leaned over. "What does it do to people?"

Yuri locked eyes. "It bypasses the ears. It goes through muscle and blood, and finds the mind directly."

Selene's heart thundered in her chest. Yuri compressed the tone to the audible range. A hollow, cathedral-like chord pulsed from the speakers, vibrating the floor. Selene took a step back, hands balling into fists. It wasn't a scream of collapse. It was the child's body finding another way forward—subsonic resonance of self-repair, beyond their language.

¶

Part 3: Echoes of a Misfire

Selene spun the floating scan beneath the lab's fluorescent tubes. Alien bone structures gleamed white with resonance mapping data. It was Rohen...or what he had been.

The doctors had called it a "Resonance Disruption Event." Minor. Traumatic. Contained. They had been lying!

Her Dawn Physiology archivist friend had leaked her the raw data files. Selene magnified her view. The sternum was not cracked but stretched, cartilage bulked—not damage but remodeling. The same in the spine, between L5 and the sacrum. A clean edge was forming a new vertebra. No cancer, no defect, no disease, just growth.

No human mutation, no accident would bring about such uniformity. It was an alteration.

She initiated a morphometric comparison. Two matches: Dawn telepathic cranial expansion blueprints, Virelian spine curving nodes for similar synaptic growth.

Her heartbeat drummed in her ears. Rohen's body had responded to an external stimulus before his mind could process. The resonance was not a scream but a warning bell.

"His body got there first."

And then the thought that stopped her: What if Ansel's body is ready for that same stimulus—and this time there's no malfunction?

¶

Part 4: Ansel's Quiet Reaction

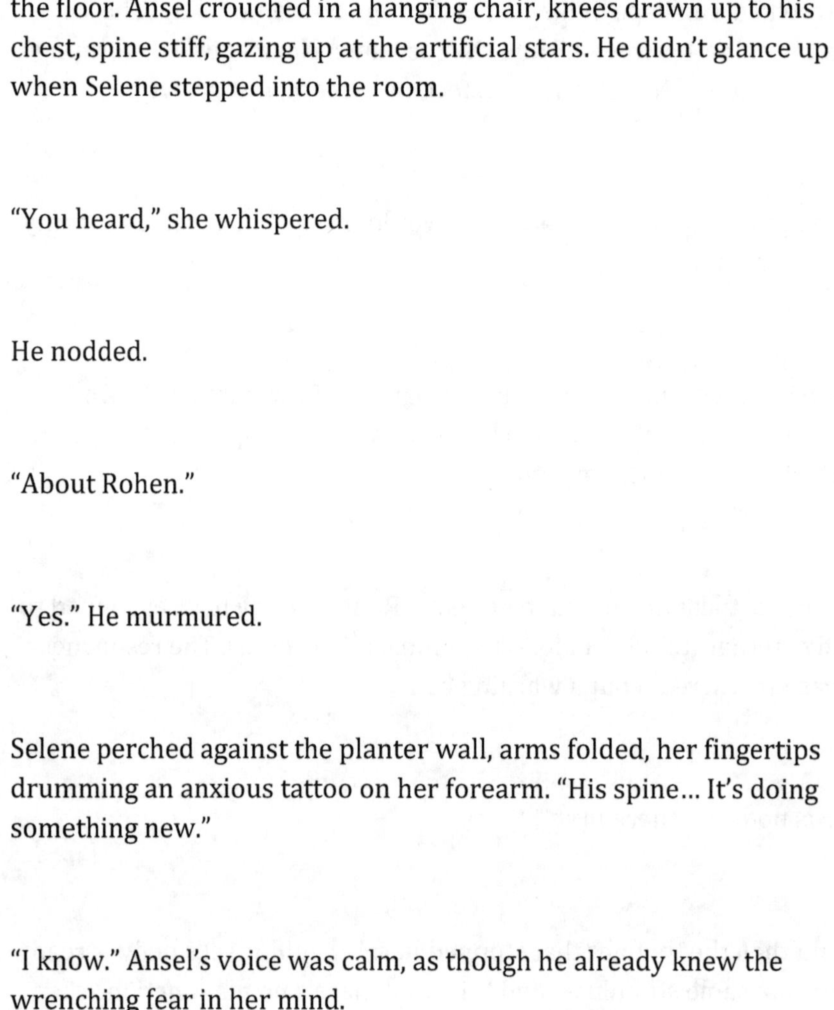

It was night, and the solarium was dark. Thin vines running across the ceiling flared dusty violet, casting long, twitching shadows across the floor. Ansel crouched in a hanging chair, knees drawn up to his chest, spine stiff, gazing up at the artificial stars. He didn't glance up when Selene stepped into the room.

"You heard," she whispered.

He nodded.

"About Rohen."

"Yes." He murmured.

Selene perched against the planter wall, arms folded, her fingertips drumming an anxious tattoo on her forearm. "His spine… It's doing something new."

"I know." Ansel's voice was calm, as though he already knew the wrenching fear in her mind.

"She convulsed." Selene fired back. "There was a frequency coming from their bones. It wasn't growth…it was a break."

He shifted, unfazed, speaking as though he was only discussing the weather. "Early sequencing."

Selene felt her heart rate spike. "Early what?"

Silently, he rose and moved across to her. "When our bodies mature before our minds can catch up, they improvise. They experiment. Sometimes things go wrong."

Selene's gaze darted to the glowing vines. "So Rohen's body ran ahead of their brain."

"Yes. It couldn't wait."

Ansel ran a fingertip over a vine; its glow flared. "Mine is waiting," he said.

Selene moved to him, close, breathing softly. "You feel it?"

He pressed a hand to his chest, then the base of his neck and nodded.

"You didn't tell me because...?"

He locked eyes with her, sorrow softening his face. "I was afraid you would want to stop it."

Selene sighed, her shoulders shaking. "Would that be wrong?"

He shook his head slowly. "I don't know if you could. And if you did...I wouldn't make it."

¶

Part 5: The Fracture Map

The lab's air felt sharper tonight, as if the temperature itself was trying to warn her. Overhead fluorescents hummed in half-light, casting long, bluish shadows across the stainless--steel benches. Selene paused by the console, fingers trembling slightly as she slid the hood of her lab coat up over her hair. Then she darkened the room to a muted half-tone and began entering her old neural passcodes—strings of sigils from the Pre--Integration Era, buried in a sandboxed vault she'd sworn never to open again.

Each digit and symbol sparked a memory: electric corridors of data she'd walked a decade ago, now dusty corridors she wasn't supposed to traverse. But necessity outweighed protocol. She breached her own firewall, navigated past school logs and public assessments, straight into the one archive no one else knew existed: Ansel's private dataset, assembled in secret since the instant he drew his first breath.

On the holo-screen, icons shimmered:

- Thirty--eight full neurological scans, each a pale ghost of branching synapses.
- Eighteen skeletal growth timelines, like the rings of a hidden tree.
- Five unprocessed bone--marrow overlays, veins, and tissue rendered in ghostly translucence.

She had not dared to open them in years. Now, with a single tap, every file erupted across the console in a latticework of data streams. She linked them all to the fracture map she'd extracted after Rohen's incident. A moment of computation, then the overlay bloomed before her: two anatomical ghosts superimposed and... perfect.

Rohen's resonance spikes—those jagged violet blips chilling enough to crack bone—lined up exactly with weak echoes in Ansel's earliest scans. Stress--point clusters she'd studied for months fell onto his cartilage like identical constellations. His vertebrae's subtle swell matched, only quieter, more diffused, as if in slumber.

Selene's breath caught. This alone was enough to freeze a soul—but there was more. She flicked to a deep--tissue capture from six months earlier, recorded after what had been labeled a "minor sports injury." The 3D bones and fascia appeared, white and pale against the dark grid. There, half-hidden at the base of his spine, flickered a third sacral marker—small, underdeveloped, a blip she'd logged as a simple calcification anomaly. Back then, she had noted it, filed it away, and moved on.

Now she ran the same predictive model she'd used to isolate Rohen's spinal mutation. Her systems hummed, then spat out the verdict in stark, mechanical lettering:

RESULT: MATCH (87%)
Classification: Controlled Structural Integration / Pre-Phase

Neural Anchorage Detected
Sequence Status: ACTIVE

Selene staggered back, pressing her palm to the cool wall as her breathing shallowed. He hadn't mentioned it because she had never seen it, though she had scanned him top to toe in digital detail. She'd combed through every pixel and data point and still missed the thing that mattered most.

Hands shaking, she initiated a full-body rendering. The lab's center crackled to life: Ansel's skeleton glowed in soft blue lines, hazy and half-formed. His skull arched into an elegant dome. His ribs curved like the hull of a ship. His spine—already beginning to curl and coil in unnatural geometry—seemed alive, as if it were knitting itself anew.

He looked less like a boy and more like a structure mid--construction. Beautiful. And terrifying.

The silence pressed in until Selene's voice cracked it open. "What are you, Ansel?" Her words echoed oddly, bouncing off steel and glass.

In answer, the neural--resonance model began to pulse. A low, sympathetic vibration hummed through the projection, tiny waves of light chasing each other down his vertebrae.

Then the console chimed—no spoken words, but a line of text appearing in a discrete corner of the display. A message she had never typed, never sanctioned, hidden in the scan data's deepest code:

"You knew. Before you forgot. That's why he chose you."

Selene's blood turned to ice. It wasn't just that she'd missed it. She had agreed to it. Her own instruments bore witness to the promise she'd made—and the choice Ansel had quietly forced upon her.

§

Chapter 7: Virel-Adran's Garden

¶

Part 1: The Living Garden

The air-ferry coasted in along the jagged coast, the ion-drive sighing under the hull. Selene leaned on the railing of the viewing deck, staring at the spiral terraces cut into the bare cliffs. She'd nearly turned around twice, but no one was left to ask her back.

The line between rock and life was indistinct. Curving walls of living stone swept out in frozen ripples of coral. Concealing the enclave of Virel-Adran. No gates, no doors, no bars. Only intent. When the ferry touched down on a cushiony mat of biolayer, its landing struts dipped, and the platform retracted from under her boots, sucking in her departure as if it were a breath.

A curtain of vines to one side was peeled back, and a narrow strip of bioluminescent moss. Its dim green light blinked beneath her feet. Selene hesitated, inhaled the air of salt and spiced bark with a hint of ozone in its breath, like the forest exhaling a dream. Stepping forward onto the trail.

Petals sprang open before her, exhaling a puff of air. Her biosense band blinked, showing empathic resonance detected. No aggressive intent—only curiosity. Towering trees spiraled toward the heavens, branches curling in mute arabesques. One of the lower branches hung heavy with fat, humming fruit, its vibrations a wash of memory. As she passed, she caught a flash of an image at the corner of her eye, a laughing Virelian child in a silvered sky. A heartbeat flash, and it was gone.

The path forked ahead. One limb curled down toward a mirror-still pool, the other curled up against a wall of thornless ivy. The green tangle of branches shuddered and pulled back, revealing a secret passage. Pull. Instinct nudged her forward—and the moss trail behind her snapped shut, blossoms sealing against her. No turning back.

Beneath the ivy arch, the light splintered into moving greens and golds. Warmth poured from the moss around her feet, alive and inviting. Selene's pulse quickened, not with apprehension but with recognition. By the time she reached the center of the glade, she knew: the garden was less a path through rock and foliage than a living echo of her own unvoiced desires. The trail before her was not leading her forward—it was leading her home.

¶

Part 2: The Language of Growth

He had been waiting for her.

Virel-Adran stood in the clearing's center, one hand against a whorled branch, gleaming like wet glass. The tree leaned into him—not by the wind, but by design.

Today, he wore no formal robes. Only a simple tunic of threadleaf and dirt-brown fabric that seemed to breathe with its own faint pulse.

"You're late," he said without opening his eyes. "Or early. Depends on which self of yours made an appearance."

Selene hesitated at the tree circle's edge. "That's always the first thing you say, and it's even more cryptic than usual."

"Is it?" He opened his eyes, then, too quickly, too wide for a man who'd just appeared to be in meditation. "We are never one person, Dr. Miro. Some justifications of self simply demand more energy."

He pointed to a thick vine that dangled from one of the lower branches. The thick rope of it curved into impossible angles, the tip rocking with purpose.

"Touch it."

"No." Selene folded her arms. "Not until you tell me why."

“Because you’ve been staring at me for two minutes and still haven’t asked why you came.” His voice sharpened. “The garden doesn’t care about that. It measures intention. It requires touch to know yours.”

Selene drew in a breath and stepped forward, taking hold of the vine. Heat surged up her arm.

The glade erupted.

Trees did not move but the space between them did, bending and reforming like reality had been coded around fixed points. Flowers snapped shut like mousetraps and then others burst into bloom with a sound like torn silk. The air grew thick with the conflict of competing scents: vanilla and blood-orange and charred wood.

The ground beneath her shook.

Selene jerked her hand away and stepped back.

The garden seized again, then became eerily still.

Virel-Adran strode around the clearing, moving with quick, deliberate steps. He touched certain blooms that seemed to pulse in response to his touch. His lips moved with noises that echoed water over stones.

"Too many possible outcomes," he said when he circled back, narrowing his eyes as if trying to look past her.

Selene clenched her jaw. "Meaning?"

"The conflict of your memories." He pointed to a cluster of flowers that had fractured into opposing colors. "The garden cannot reconcile your intentions."

"I did not come here to be reconciled." The old defiance was creeping into her voice. The same edge she'd used on their first meeting, when he'd called her research "charmingly primitive."

His mouth twisted in amusement. "Then why seek me out, Dr. Miro, after three months of silence?"

The question hung between them, heavy as the silence she had tried to avoid since Ansel had first begun speaking in harmonics last winter.

"I made a deal with someone years ago," she said finally. "And it's coming to fruition through my son, now. Through all the Dawns." Her hands balled into fists. "I need to know what I agreed to."

Virel-Adran shifted subtly in the grass—the slight stiffening she'd learned to recognize as surprise.

"You've finally come to ask what the garden was built to answer."

Selene took a step closer, close enough to smell the mineral scent of his skin. "Then answer me."

Behind them, the vines coiled and uncoiled in agitated patterns.

"The answer is not words," he said, locking eyes with her, then. "It's a memory you have long since buried. Who you were before you chose to become someone else."

¶

Part 3: The Seed and the Memory

The trail narrowed suddenly. One moment, they were in a glade of root-spires and flowering vines; the next, boughs bent in and petals closed. Selene followed Virel-Adran into a tunnel of green shadows. The light was different here—cooler, and shot with pale blue rays.

Branches twisted forward in impossible precision. Their trunks rose in perfect helices, smooth and unbroken. Veins of faintly glowing vapor wafted between them, like wayward smoke. Selene's breath caught.

The place hummed with an echo of a memory that was not her own. She touched a glowing filament—and her mind went white with the smell of grass under twin moons, a spark of glass fire, the outline of someone kneeling before her—then was blank. She gasped.

"What is this place?" Selene breathed.

Virel-Adran fell in beside her, hands clasped behind his back. "The Alvah Fold," he said. "A resonance grove. Not constructed, but cultivated. Every tree in here germinated from an unspoken memory. Most are Virelian, though some are much older."

"Older than Virelian?" Selene asked.

He only nodded.

On they walked until they came to a shallow pool with dark flowers around its rim that never bloomed. In a mossy cradle at its edge lay a seed pod, no bigger than a plum: pale and throbbing.

"What's that?" Selene murmured.

He knelt and took it in his palm. "A Dawn child's first resonance tear fell into these roots. This plant responded by producing this."

He offered it to her. Selene stepped back. As it approached, the pod throbbed twice—deep and sonorous.

Selene stammered. "What's inside?"

"Not a thought or a memory," he said. "A confirmation. Proof that what has happened once can happen again." He met her gaze. "It has no DNA or neural code, and yet its vibration is both Ansel's and yours."

She shook her head. "That can't be real."

Virel-Adran smiled a little sadly. "You believe evolution only progresses. But some things circle back. This seed is not evidence of something new—it's evidence of something old coming around again."

He set it carefully on the moss. The two of them stood in silence, as deep and still as the grove itself.

¶

Part 4: "The Seed Must Forget the Tree"

They continued to walk in silence for several steps, further into the grove's green cathedral of hushed foliage. Damp earth gave underfoot with a whisper, and the air was tinged with the smell of moss and half-remembered rain.

Above them, the lattice-work of the canopy diffused the sky, staining it a muted pre-dawn gray-blue, as though the world still lay suspended between night and day. Selene's thoughts skittered against one another like loose stones, jagged and unspoken questions lodging in her throat like thorns.

Eventually, she could not stand it. She stopped so suddenly that a loose swirl of mist billowed around her boots.

"No more riddles," she said, her voice rough with disuse, with patience already threadbare and worn. "No more botanical metaphors. I want answers."

Virel-Adran did not turn. He hovered before a spiraled trunk, whose gnarled knot glowed faintly with captured dawn-light, as though the tree itself were breathing.

"I have given you answers," he replied in a low, steady tone that seemed to rise from the roots beneath their feet. "You simply keep asking the wrong questions."

Selene's fists clenched at her sides. "I watched a seed pulse in time with my son's resonance. I deciphered messages in the curling shapes his dreaming fingers drew. You knew this would happen—you've always known."

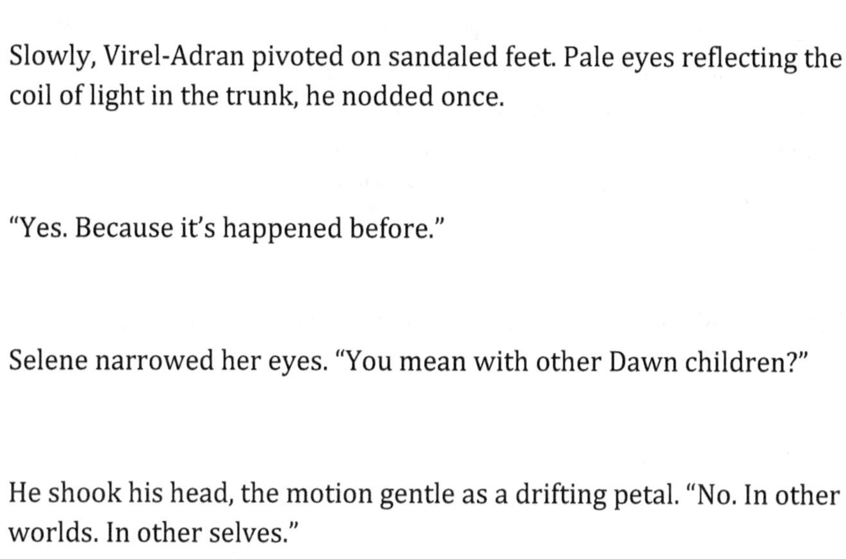

Slowly, Virel-Adran pivoted on sandaled feet. Pale eyes reflecting the coil of light in the trunk, he nodded once.

"Yes. Because it's happened before."

Selene narrowed her eyes. "You mean with other Dawn children?"

He shook his head, the motion gentle as a drifting petal. "No. In other worlds. In other selves."

A sudden breeze threaded through the grove, though no breeze should have reached this lofty place. Leaves trembled like silken curtains stirred by an unseen hand.

Selene's voice fell to a whisper. "What are the Dawns, really?"

Virel-Adran stepped forward, each footfall a hush on the soft humus. He bore no weapon, no looming menace—only a calm stillness, as if he were part of the grove itself.

"They are moments when memory returns to flesh," he said, and his words rippled through the air like a distant chant.

He swept one arm toward the spiral trees, their trunks coiled like ancient scripts. "You believe evolution is a straight path—biology's forward march. But the Dawns are not in front of you. They surround you: behind, beneath, within. You crawled from the sea, then forgot how salt tasted on your tongue. You crafted language, then forgot the music of thought unspoken."

Selene's nails bit into her palms. "Then what—what are you?"

His gaze held hers, unwavering. "I am what you will become again."

She recoiled as if struck, his voice echoing in her mind like a secret trapped in stone. "You're not aliens."

He said nothing.

"You're not visitors," she pressed on. "You're... some kind of recursion? A loop?"

His voice dropped to a hush so deep it sounded woven from the grove itself: "I am not from elsewhere. I am from after."

Selene's breath caught in her chest, the world tilting. "So you guided the Dawns, not to prepare them for tomorrow, but to remind them of the past we've all but forgotten."

Virel-Adran inclined his head, the spirals of his hair brushing his shoulder. "You call it evolution. I call it recognition. And like every memory rekindled in bone and blood, it begins clumsily—with sound, with dreams, with the slow reshaping of marrow."

He gestured to a single pod nestled in the emerald moss, its hushed shell still warm with hidden life.

"That seed remembers its origin," he murmured, "but it cannot grow if it clings to the shape of the tree that bore it."

He met her gaze then—no judgment, no sorrow—only a profound, yearning patience.

"The seed must forget the tree to grow."

¶

Part 5: Leaving the Path

Selene was alone.

Virel-Adran nodded once and disappeared into the trees. They folded shut behind him, like water lapping over rock.

She didn't want to ask for directions, not if it would tell her things she didn't want to know about herself.

The garden observed her, wordlessly. Judging her, she felt.

She followed the moss path that had promised to lead her back to the main grove—but had not. Everything was subtly different. The leaves were a deeper shade of green. The trees had changed their angles, now pointing in new directions. Fruits she remembered were blooming white and spiraled, rather than golden and starburst.

She spun slowly, feeling her heart rate climb. The path had widened, and the moss now pulsed with her heart. She turned to head back, but the curve behind her had changed.

She couldn't find the way back. Landmarks refused to be fixed as she grew more frantic.

And then she realized.

The garden wasn't shifting around her—she was. It was reacting to the person she had become. The things she'd learned, remembered, broken open inside herself.

It was not a map. It was a mirror.

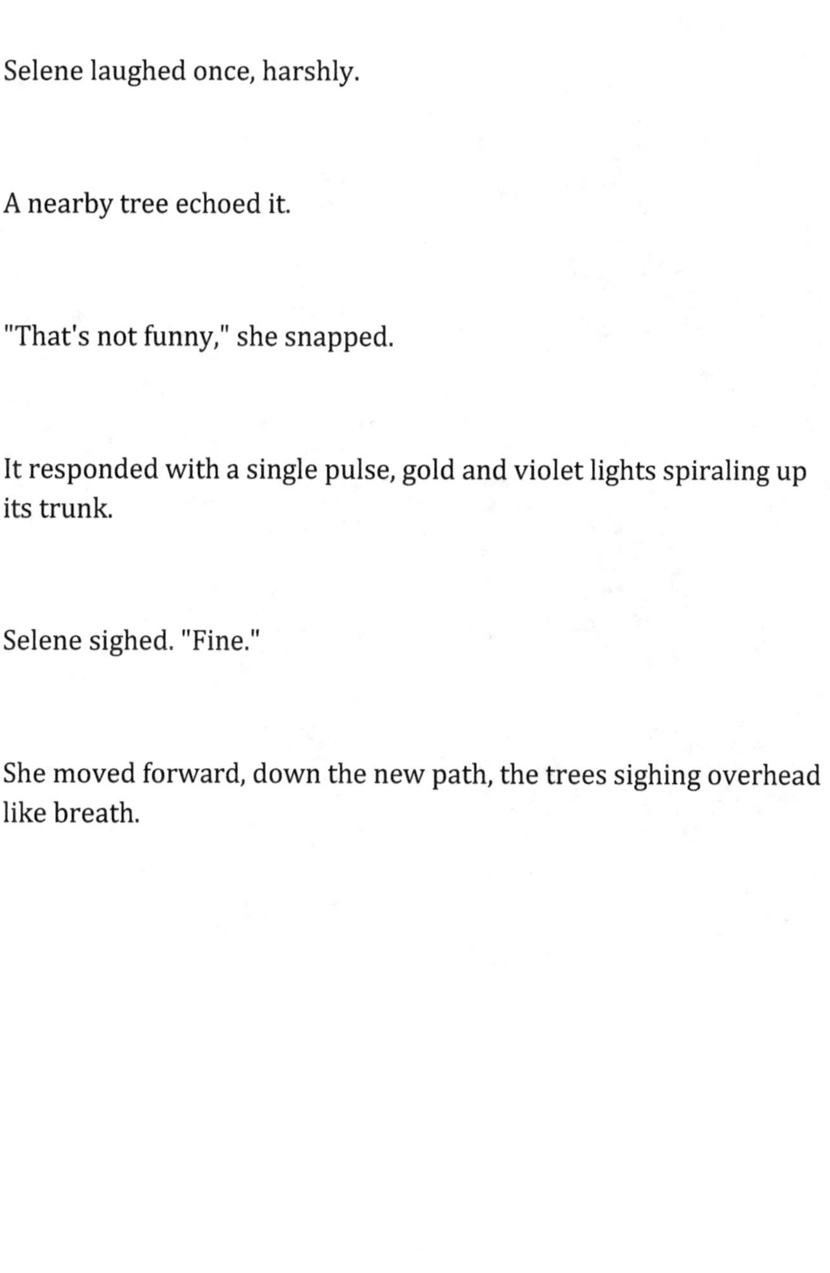

Selene laughed once, harshly.

A nearby tree echoed it.

"That's not funny," she snapped.

It responded with a single pulse, gold and violet lights spiraling up its trunk.

Selene sighed. "Fine."

She moved forward, down the new path, the trees sighing overhead like breath.

§

Chapter 8: A Language Without Words

¶

Part 1: The Sculpture Garden

The sculpture garden was on the northern ridge of the Dawn Institute, where the city dropped away below broken rooftops and entangled vines. Today, the students were here for "unstructured resonance exposure," a session in learning how to read the living stone, glass, and metal that shaped itself to the mood of the moment.

Ansel wandered the terraces in his worn gray robe, not minding the breeze whipping at the hem. His classmates huddled by morphing sculptures, some pulsing with sound, some weeping condensation. One resonite shard, however, riveted him: a blade, twisting into itself, with facets smooth and yet eerily balanced. No one knew who'd grown it, or why it hadn't moved since coming into being.

It might have been the brief tremor that coursed through the garden before he noticed, but nothing in the sculpture moved around that one piece—only, in Ansel's chest, a rising tension. He sucked in a steadying breath and closed his eyes.

Seconds.

And then the sculpture twitched, as though wakened by a forgotten memory. Light faded from its surface, and it began to absorb it, rather than reflect it. The shift was silent until a low vibration shook Ansel's teeth and settled low in his belly.

A girl not far from him writhed in sudden sobs, mouth moving in the name of someone she'd never known. A boy vomited behind a sheet of trembling steel. The shard curled into itself, atom by atom, sinking without a sound or a fissure.

Instructors arrived before anyone stirred, to find only a shallow spiral etched in the moss at Ansel's feet—the same spiral he'd drawn in the dirt of his cell every night he couldn't sleep.

He opened his eyes. There was no release, no victory. Ansel turned on silent feet and left the space, watched by students who still stared at the place where something real had simply unraveled itself.

¶

Part 2: The Teacher's Report

Selene read it three times.

She sat at her desk in the darkened lab. The only light was the hazy glow of the holo-display, which shimmered like a mirage in time with the pulse of the message. It throbbed slowly, breathing in the silence.

FROM: Instructor Aeth Lerna

SUBJECT: Field Report — Incident 223F: Garden Resonance Disruption

Dr. Miro,

I am reporting this incident as observational, rather than as an emergency. I have requested a consensus board review, nonetheless.

During today's unstructured resonance exposure period, student Ansel Miro initiated an unspoken, unmeasured resonance event in the sculpture garden. There was no evidence of physical contact. The resonite structure underwent complete spontaneous dissolution, classified as implosive molecular reversion.

There was no known external device or augmentation on the student's person.

Nine other students present in the area experienced the following within 90 seconds of the event:

- **Two began to sob, with no apparent reason.**
- **One student laughed hysterically and inquired, "Didn't you feel the old rain?"**
- **Four students reported the appearance of unidentifiable faces.**
- **One student entered a catatonic state for 2.3 minutes before reciting a poem in an apparently non-existent dialect.**

All students are physically stable. Emotive volatility is rated Level 3 (contained).

Ansel's only remark when questioned was as follows:

"I didn't speak. I remembered."

Several other students, later independently and unprompted, approached us to say,

"He said something without saying it."

Please advise.

Selene opened the garden's sensor feeds. Brows sharp and focused, she skimmed through the steady data stream. No voice spike. No localized kinetic activity. She glanced at Ansel, waiting, and then saw it: one long, low, complex pulse, arcing across the entire resonance mesh in perfect synchronicity.

A harmonic without a source. Not from Ansel's voice, or hands, or the ground. It was coming from everywhere around him at once.

Words from the official report echoed in her mind. "I didn't speak. I remembered."

She closed the file. The implications swam through her head. This was no communication, no asking or receiving. This was imposition. Whatever he did, whatever it was that he 'remembered', it simply appeared in the minds of everyone around him at once. No asking for permission, or even explaining. Just taking over and forcing a single thought to become a reality without translation.

¶

Part 3: The Resonant Thread

The lab was so quiet that Selene could hear the soft thrum of the mapping rig. Ansel sat perfectly still, sensors glistening on his scalp. She remembered his fidgeting energy, his constant questions—so different from this stillness.

Selene clicked through the standard speech-prep checks—jaw tension, breath shifts, and the brain activity they'd come to expect. Nothing. The blank readout left her feeling hollow.

She swallowed and loaded the footage from the sculpture's collapse, switching to a deeper resonance filter. The screen shimmered, then blossomed into a smooth braid of light, curling softly at its center. It wasn't the jagged spike of an EEG readout or the steady ebb and flow of a heartbeat— it was purposeful, almost rhythmic.

Her heart pounded in her chest. That form…she had seen it in forbidden archives, traces of an ancestral language encoded in pure vibration. Trembling, she overlaid the two readouts. They were far too similar to be a coincidence.

Heart still racing, Selene turned back to Ansel, her voice a whisper. "Ansel… was that you?"

His eyes flickered open, clear and still. After a moment, he gave her a small, steady smile. "I wasn't trying to communicate. I was remembering how it feels when nothing is separate."

¶

Part 4: Thought as Environment

She flicked a switch, and the lab went dark. Screens off. No charts, no pulses, no harmonics. Just him.

Ansel was sitting cross-legged on the floor. Barefoot. The shirt was ragged and slipping off one shoulder. Eyes half-lidded—old and new in the same gaze. She slid in beside him, back against the moss-covered wall.

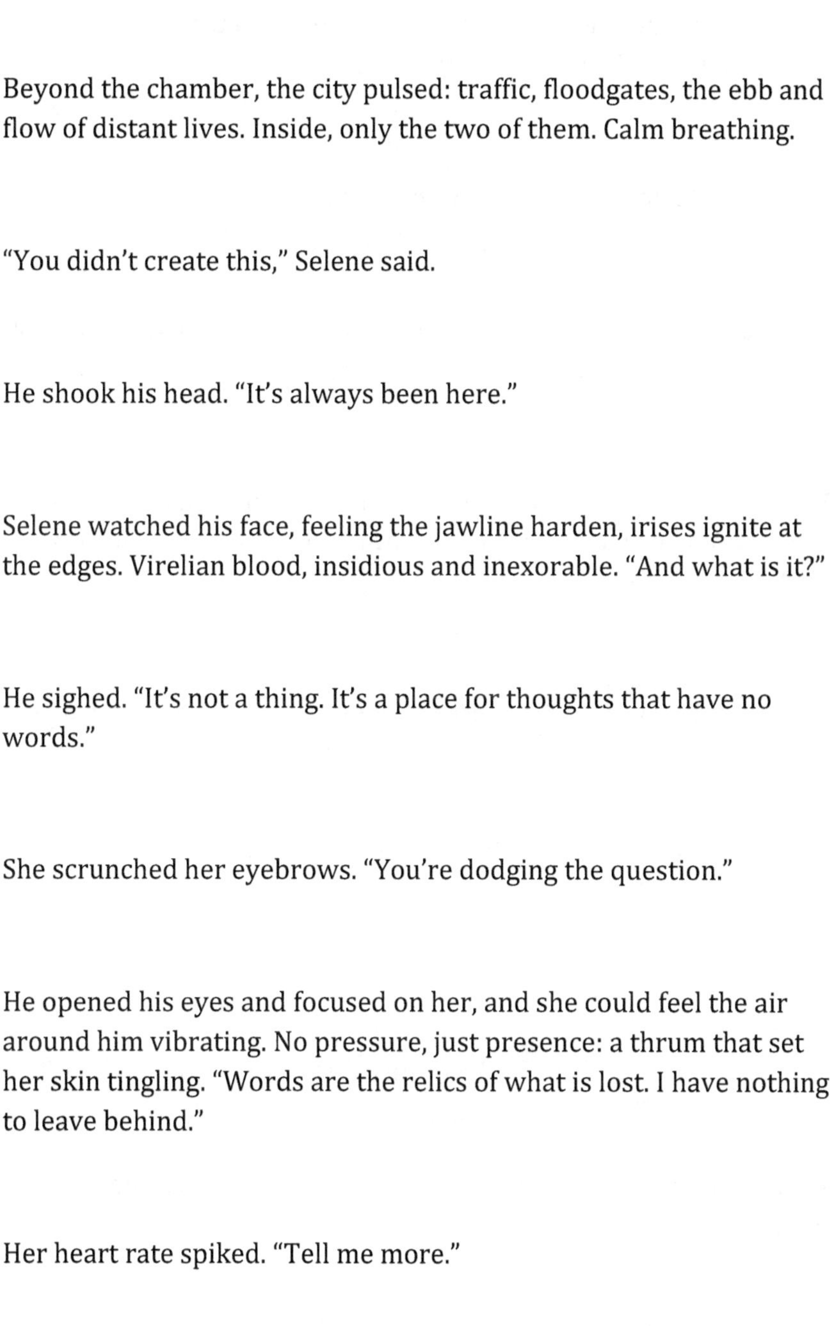

Beyond the chamber, the city pulsed: traffic, floodgates, the ebb and flow of distant lives. Inside, only the two of them. Calm breathing.

“You didn’t create this,” Selene said.

He shook his head. “It’s always been here.”

Selene watched his face, feeling the jawline harden, irises ignite at the edges. Virelian blood, insidious and inexorable. “And what is it?”

He sighed. “It’s not a thing. It’s a place for thoughts that have no words.”

She scrunched her eyebrows. “You’re dodging the question.”

He opened his eyes and focused on her, and she could feel the air around him vibrating. No pressure, just presence: a thrum that set her skin tingling. “Words are the relics of what is lost. I have nothing to leave behind.”

Her heart rate spiked. “Tell me more.”

He was silent for a beat, then she felt it in her chest. A burst of heat, suffocating and intimately familiar: hospital corridor, palms sweating with urgency, partner's life hanging by a thread. She inhaled sharply. "That's not my memory."

He gazed into her eyes. "It is your core. It is mine."

Selene's hand shot to her mouth. He hadn't told her. He'd shown her. Raw and unprocessed.

Ansel's smile was faint. "I was expressing emotion, not statements. Thought can be an experience: a breath, a heartbeat, the darkness behind closed eyes."

Selene leaned toward him, voice cracking. "This… it's not language."

He blinked, then closed his eyes. "It's pre-language."

¶

Part 5: The Spiral Bloom

It danced before the console—misty strands of helices in slow, methodical orbits.

Selene had repurposed Ansel's resonance spike into a biosonic visualization. A data-analysis technique adopted by cultural artists and cult philosophers to transcribe sub-audio schema into fluid morphologies.

The waveform oscillated, trembled, then bloated. It unfurled like a nebula, collapsed inward, and reformed. An iteration fractal, but non-random.

Selene inched forward, pupils expanding. There was something voyeuristic about it. As if the image possessed eyes and was staring at the back of her head.

The software generated a label:

Dynamic Behavioral Attractor
Status: Unresolved Memory Cluster
Host Identity: Inferred
Confidence Score: 92%
Assigned Host: Miro, Selene

Her knuckles whitened against the console's edge. The attractor had identified her—not Ansel—as the intended host. It wasn't just data. It was a memory reaching out for its host.

"No," she hissed.

There was a sensation in her core—a pulse long deadened, a twinge just behind her sternum. Foreign, yet familiar. As if she'd come across a fragment of herself she'd consciously misplaced.

Selene snapped the visualization shut. Black swarmed in. Silence filled her ears.

The black screen flickered once, rendering a single, translated word:

"Welcome back."

Part 1: The Declassified Signal

§

Chapter 9: A War That Never Was

¶

Part 1: The Declassified Signal

The decryption was 100%. Selene cracked her knuckles on the antique neural pad—it couldn't be hacked, thank God.

She leaned in as the screen gave her access:

PROJECT: VERA-SIGN
BLACK VAULT / VIEW ONLY
DATE: EARTH—Y+1 PRE-CONTACT

Static buzzed out to reveal a grainy video. A timestamp. 75 years past. The camera zoomed in on the face of a thin technician, wearing a Deep-Signal Array uniform, glaring into the lens.

"We've found something. Not a message. It's... us," she breathed out.

The screen warped to a thick, pulsing waveform, organic and in rhythm with the neural rest frequency of the planet. It was broadcasting, but not information. It was listening—waiting for a handshake on its echo.

The video ended. Another file, smaller and older, played alone.

Selene gulped and hit play.

"Hello. If you're receiving this, it means they're out there—or you've let them out. Either way. You were right not to trust, wrong to fear. They're not here for us. They're here for what we lost. They're already here. We just haven't woken up yet." Her partner's tired voice spoke from the lab, from behind her.

A click, and the file cut off.

Selene leaned back in her chair, heart heavy. The signal had not alerted. Had not declared. It had simply held a mirror to Earth—and humanity had already turned the damn key.

¶

Part 2: The Cities That Prepared to Burn

The second file came in pixels of corrupted data and grayscale. This was not surveillance footage. This was a military intelligence report, compiled from spy satellites and encrypted local feeds. Much of it had never been declassified before this moment.

Selene's eyes scanned as the images played:

New Delhi, 02:37 UTC
Traffic jams on highways, choked with fleeing vehicles. People vanish into underground bunkers. Anti-aircraft guns mounted on building roofs, barrels pointed up.

Berlin, 04:02 UTC
Airport activity shut down; all internet traffic is rerouted to hardline dead zones. Digital displays flash: "Initiate neural screening. Archive access prohibited."

Denver, 23:16 Local
Interceptor aircraft launch. Underground train tunnels are closed. A monotone speaker announces: "Prepare for atmospheric breach, visual distortion, psychological immersion."

Tokyo. Cairo. São Paulo. Reykjavik.
Metropoles all over the world turn inward, steeling themselves against something more than conventional warfare.

She'd seen it a thousand times in training exercises—decades of drills distilled into a few rapid scenes. This was not a defensive formation. This was a full-scale occupation.

The projection shifts to meeting transcripts and wargames, models calculating body counts under various "atmospheric penetration" outcomes. Then there was one report that caught her attention:

SIMULATION 09R – LIKELY ALIEN ENGINAGEMENT
RESULT: GLOBAL CATASTROPHE < 48 HOURS
ACTION: PSYCHOLOGICAL HARDENING TO DELAY CAPITULATION

Selene pressed her lips together. "Capitulation?" she mumbled. There was no mention of weapon counts—only "semantic resilience" and defenses against "untranslatable cognitive superiority."

The human race wasn't preparing for an attack on ships or ICBMs. They were steeling themselves for an attack on thought itself.

Then the transmission ended. No invasion. No detonations. No breach—only a sudden silence.

Weeks later, the Virelians came. They did not arrive in droves, nor did they make any declaration. They simply materialized at the outskirts of our cities, ghostlike, as if they had never left.

Selene put her hands on her head, thinking back to those preparations. The human race had prepared for a fire—and found only ashes.

¶

Part 3: The Offer Without Terms

The file opened to black. The screen blinked on, without fanfare, without alert. No warning. No encrypted prompt.

Only a title, in an alien script, formed of filigreed glyphs that throbbed with cold, milky radiance:

"Memory in Absence."

The footage started immediately.

The room was circular, its low basalt vault streaked with vents that sighed with the soft rasp of hidden machinery. The filtered light of amber suns cut across its height through angled apertures, throwing motes of dust into lazy eddies like wandering spirits. A biomesh table hovered in its centre, grown of organic fibre and luminous with a steady, thready pulse. Twelve people were seated at the table: generals in starched uniforms, diplomats in muted silks, neurophilosophers whose eyepieces flashed. Some of them wore thin translation visors; others shut their eyes, steeling themselves in silence.

At the table's head, however, was the first Virelian that had ever been documented on Earth. Their body were lithe, their skin a smooth opal that shone with pearlescent reflections in the dim light. Filamentous tendrils curled against their forearms and draped across their midsection with elegant repose. They breathed not, spoke not a greeting. The Virelian's eyes—if that was what they were—sleek and oblique and unblinking, watched through a plane not quite recognizable by the camera.

The Virelian unclasped one hand and extended a long, bony finger. They dipped it into the hollow of their side and brought a single living bloom into the air. It hovered in their palm: translucent petals trembling with gentle bioluminescence, ribbed with arteries of biothread. A scent like petrichor on cracked stone drifted from it. Without a word, they placed the bloom upon the biomesh table.

It unfurled itself without a sound, petals spreading like the slow heartbeat of a nova. Selene sat with her spine straight with attention. The camera feed warped; the table, the room, the humans evaporated into raw sensation.

Now the footage showed a holographic neural field. Every sensation was transmitted in unwanted neural echoes: a scorched world under the twin gaze of unforgiving suns, the air so hot it writhed with animate entropy. Then the cool caress of a foreign hand, cupping the clay and releasing it grain by grain, each a small tumble through shaking fingers. A voice, alone and trembling, uttering a name in a coarse, throaty language that clung to the larynx—an elegy to loss. And, finally, a horizon of white dust so long undisturbed it was holy in its emptiness.

No voiceover. No subtitles. Nothing but exile, distilled.

And then, at last, a vision of Earth. A vulnerable sphere of blue and green marbled with absence and made ghostly by the trickle of memory that wove itself back toward its continents.

The vision ended. The room reassembled. Silence reasserted itself. Words inscribed in the bloom's own symbology and translated into all the alphabets of humankind shimmered on the screen:

"We are not asking. We are remembering. If you are still who we were, then you already understand."

Selene's fingers twitched over the console. She closed the file. The glyphs dimmed.

It was not peace. It was not conquest. It was not even an invitation.

It was an inheritance.

¶

Part 4: Prototype Zero

The hidden file, when found, was more deeply buried than any other.

Selene had signed into her personal account using the private passcode that she hadn't used since the day Ansel was born: a random string of numbers she had long ago forgotten. Forgotten, that is, until today. Today, it unlocked far more than a file.

The file, somehow, was doing more than just fighting to decrypt. It was fighting to be found, as well. When at last it did appear, it was with a header that filled her entire screen:

PROJECT ID: THETA-PROTO // PHASE ZERO
SECURITY LEVEL: NONDISCLOSURE / NONTEMPORAL
KEY NAMES: Miro, Eren – Chief Theorist (Deceased)
SUBJECT: Hybrid Lineage Initiation — PRE-CONTACT PHASE

Selene's stomach dropped. Eren—her partner she'd lost and Ansel's other parent—was listed here like they had been waiting for this day.

The screen flipped to detailed schematics: the double helix, laced with the same spiraling neuro-lattices she had first seen when Ansel's first genome was scanned and again when Rohen's physical was being coded. Her breath caught on the date, however:

DATE: Y–3 EARTH STANDARD

Three years, full years, before any Virelian ship had been "discovered."

"No," Selene murmured, shaking her head. "That's not possible."

She had assumed, somehow, that the neural lattice patterns in the genome were a byproduct of first contact. But these files were irrefutable evidence that the patterns had, in fact, been there all along, embedded and inert within the human genome itself.

A built-in audio file began, Eren's voice soft and halting.

"We don't know what causes these things. We don't know how they're triggered. But we do know they're not mutations. They're recalls. Harmonic field exposure doesn't change stem cells. It reminds them. It's not evolution. It's remembering."

Selene swallowed hard. He knew, then. Knew before they had even been discovered. Knew before the first Virelian had even descended. Knew, and watched the genome, and said nothing.

Raw fury, and then a piercing grief, tore through her. All these years, when he had comforted her as she sobbed into their shoulder in fear of what Ansel's initial scan had found, they had been lying to her. Or lying to himself. It all made sense, now, the way they had looked at their son: not as a child with features to be denied, but a child, a new life, whose genetic memory was a signal that Eren had known about from the very beginning.

She remembered the name they had given him, Ansel, "protected by the gods." Protection. Shield. A safeguard. A signal. Or perhaps a beacon, waiting for the world to catch up.

Tears fell as Selene looked at the screen again. She had lost so much. Her partner. Her reason for having children at all. Her own sense of identity.

But beneath all that, another emotion was beginning to rise, tiny, bright, dangerous. Curiosity.

Ansel wasn't a miracle, not just for her. He was a sign, proof of something humanity had thought it had forgotten. And she couldn't look away.

¶

Part 5: The War That Never Was

The filename flickered on Selene's screen:

COUNCIL BRIEF 0-Alpha / Witness Footage / Final Deliberation.

She hit "play."

The feed stabilized to a still shot of a cavernous stone room—thirteen human delegates seated around a polished obsidian table, three Virelians standing rigid at their sides. No emblems, no titles, no interpreters. The shoulders of the delegates hunched under the throbbing lights. A storm crashed against the glass walls beyond, but the sound of the wind never penetrated the room.

There was silence for a moment, save for the quiet click of a microphone.

General Alene Dray broke the stillness with a voice sharp and measured, "We have studied your memory-seeds and weighed your proposals. But peace with no sovereignty is slavery. You speak of conversion, not coexistence. This is an invasion, not negotiation."

One of the Virelians stepped forward. Its skin undulated in darker blues, each pulsing wave like a tide pulling back. It spoke with a voice that Selene found both soothing and unsettling—utterly genderless, velvety smooth, but strangely resonant in the throat: "You cannot be taken."

Dray's mouth tightened. "That is not a denial."

The alien blinked slowly as if timing its breaths with some otherworldly pulse and repeated, "You cannot be taken. Only remembered."

Selene saw a flicker of uncertainty across several of the humans' faces. Dray continued, "We choose for ourselves, not you."

"But you chose"—the Virelian's voice dropped to a whisper—"to forsake yourselves long before we came. You choose again now, through us, with us, as us."

Minister Tejani leaned in, his voice unsteady. "Then where is the war we were warned of? The one you would not fight?"

The Virelian cocked its head to one side, the blues in its skin fading into one serene hue. "The war is over. You simply never learned who won."

The feed went black. No final vote. No document signed. Just silence.

Selene shuddered out a breath. Her fingers went numb on the console. She stared at the empty room on her screen, at the stilled faces of humanity's finest—some ashen with disbelief, others looking past it all into some unnamable void.

The decision had not been on any treaty. The true fight was never over a battle, but over memory itself. And forgetting had already been defeated.

§

Chapter 10: Whispers in the Lattice

¶

Part 1: The Scan That Doesn't Fade

It started as a twinge in her stomach. Selene wasn't searching. She was just cycling through Ansel's oldest files, scanning for some detail she might have missed, some imperfection she could use. A bug. A vulnerability. Something to put off the inevitable for another day.

She pulled up **File 000-MIRO-A**—Ansel, at five weeks. She'd watched it so many times her brain should have processed the view count, but there it was: pristine. He'd stretched still in the imaging hammock, eyes bright and open. "He already knows," the technician had told her, offhandedly. An unguarded comment. She felt like it had been a warning now.

The brain scan unfurled across the display in flawless resolution, each crease and surge as detailed as when they'd first been captured. No static. No corruption. Nothing. Just flawless data, refusing to decay.

Integrity: 100 percent.
Degradation: 0.00 percent.
Last Accessed: Never.

Selene's heart hammered in her chest. How could a file she'd unearthed dozens of times not even register her presence? The system had wiped her access out, without a single footprint behind.

Selene pressed back in her chair, jaw clenched. Was the file protecting itself? Or someone else muddying its past?

"By what?" Selene whispered to the machine's whir.

Silence. Nothing but the persistent fluorescence of an old memory, too well preserved to be real:

Some memories aren't in you.
Some live through you.

¶

Part 2: Beneath the Noise Floor

She pulled the switch. The console darkened, glowing deeper orange as the deep-frame filter engaged. A digital sieve coded for only the strangest anomaly hunting. Born to map unknown cognition in comatose patients, to visualize not audio but intent sewn into neuro-resonant static. Many had cast it aside as too ethereal, its output dissipating like sunlight through fog. Selene didn't care if it was real.

She focused on the raw trace. The very moment Ansel's temporal lobe first sparked to life. Five weeks into gestation, it should have registered only reflexive body twitching. Instead, the data was shockingly crisp, as if thought itself was crystallizing in the air.

Her hand flicked the threshold slider to the lowest click.

Human hearing can detect about twenty hertz. She dropped it further. To sixteen.

The console hiccupped, then sighed out a low mournful groan—no musical note but thick pressure thrumming like a heartbeat stamped into thick velvet. The sub-audio frequency thrummed through her skeleton.

Selene blinked. Behind that growl, a voice came.

It wasn't Ansel's infantile coo. It wasn't even her own voice. It was close and far away at once, like the residue of a conversation she used to have in a now locked-away room.

A rasp breathed her name: "...**Selene**..."

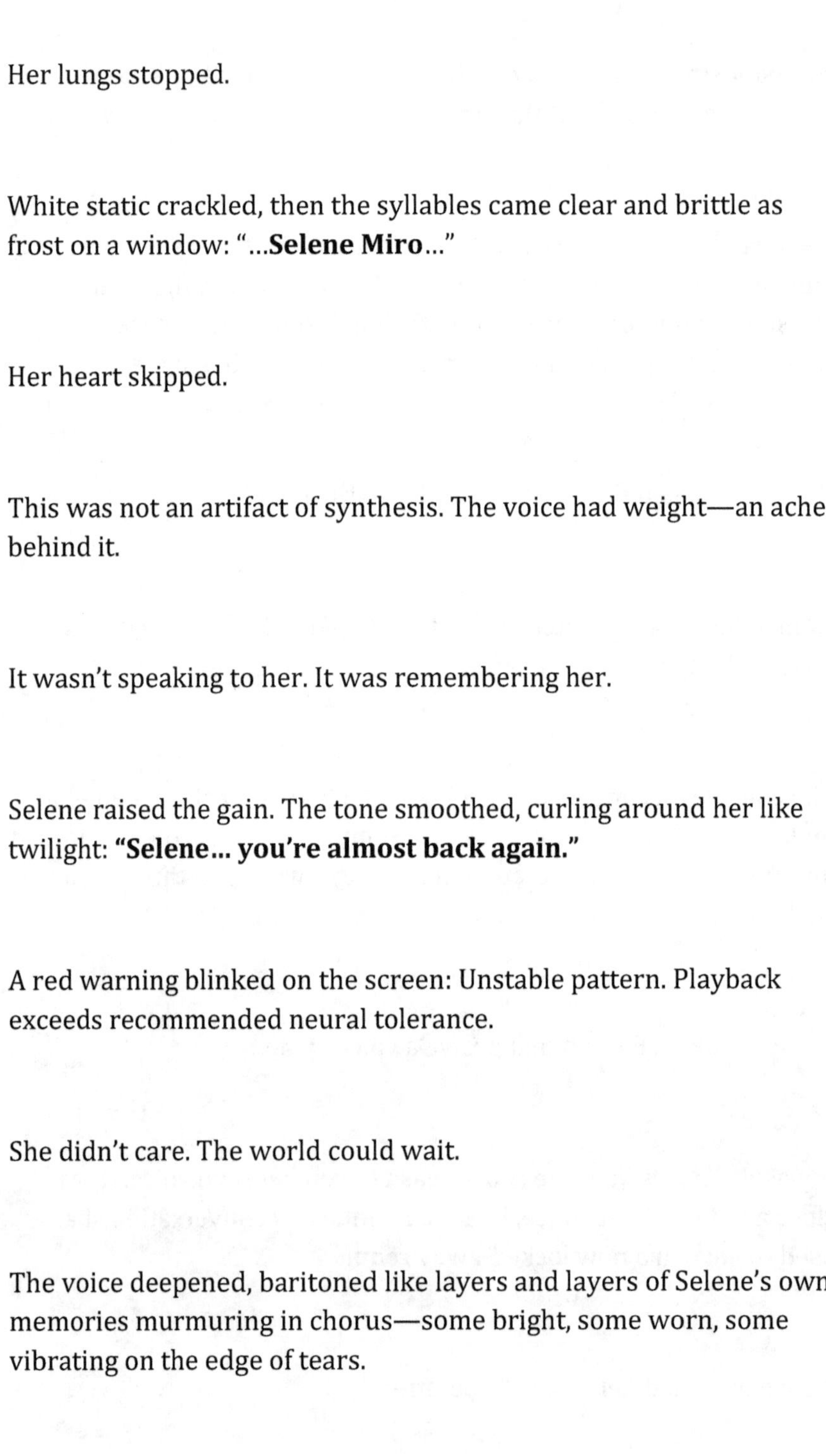

Her lungs stopped.

White static crackled, then the syllables came clear and brittle as frost on a window: "...**Selene Miro**..."

Her heart skipped.

This was not an artifact of synthesis. The voice had weight—an ache behind it.

It wasn't speaking to her. It was remembering her.

Selene raised the gain. The tone smoothed, curling around her like twilight: **"Selene... you're almost back again."**

A red warning blinked on the screen: Unstable pattern. Playback exceeds recommended neural tolerance.

She didn't care. The world could wait.

The voice deepened, baritoned like layers and layers of Selene's own memories murmuring in chorus—some bright, some worn, some vibrating on the edge of tears.

Then it was quiet and loud at the same time: **"Do you remember the first forgetting?"**

Her throat closed off. The lab air seemed to squeeze around her—walls throbbing with fluorescent heat, machines exhaling like held breath.

This voice was not recorded in the scan. It was under it, as if the raw data were a casing, and the true something had been growing in silence under her, biding time until someone listened hard enough in the quiet.

¶

Part 3: Recursive Echoes

The voice didn't repeat.

That was the first thing she thought after it looped a third time.

The voice changed. A little. Not in what it said, but in how. In cadence.

First, it said, **"Selene...you're almost back."**

Then, **"Selene Miro. You are still the echo I carried."**

On the fifth iteration, **"I remember you before you chose forgetting."**

Selene's spine went cold. It wasn't a loop. It was an iteration.

It knew she was listening. Something watched her, listening to her listening. Every loop unlocked a deeper level of analysis, as if the scan was tuned not for her ears but for her mental state.

She activated empathic pair mode, the parapathic tool mapping her physiological betrayal: pupils dilated, fingertip temperature dropping, cortisol peaking and crashing. Her hippocampus's memory nodes are lighting up with each iteration.

"This isn't a recording," she said softly. The words came into being in her chest before she consciously thought them. She was not listening—she was being read.

On the eighth iteration, the voice was whole, singular, undeniable: **"You weren't supposed to remember. But you're remembering beautifully."**

Selene reeled away from the interface. The voice had become not a sound outside herself but an echo within—recovery as knowing that comes before language, before identity. Phrases breached her more deeply, each word more hers.

The scan was not sending her information. It was making something with her.

¶

Part 4: A Signature Woven in Thought

Selene inhaled, forcing her heart to calm. The voice in her head didn't stop echoing. Not in a way that sounded like a voice—more a pressure, a dull throb against her temples. She needed to know for certain.

Selene initialized a resonance trace, dissecting the scan's audio channel into neural harmonic clusters. Too complex for static, too methodical for an infant's rambling. She isolated the enigmatic signature:

SOURCE: UNKNOWN
AUTH: NOT ANSEL
STABILITY: 87%

No genetic material, no developmental signatures—nothing. It hadn't been Ansel. It had been spliced into Ansel's scan. She searched the lab's archived records—years before Virelian filters became the standard. One match:

MIRO, EREN. NEURAL DEPARTURE LOG: POSITIVE RES-TRACE.

Her partner. Ansel's other parent. Classified as fragmented following initial hybrid resonance testing, and then disappeared. Selene's hand shook as she opened Eren's departure log.

It was not a recording. It was a fractal—a chaotic knot of harmonics nearly identical to what she had found hiding in Ansel's scan, but rawer, and saturated with loss. Eren's mind hadn't died. It had replicated itself.

The console blinked, then the scan reloaded. Softer now, the voice murmured in her head:

"You thought you were bringing him into the world. But you were the one who was born. You were built to carry me forward. Not as a mother. As a vector."

Selene staggered back, heart pounding. This wasn't a farewell message. It was a live signature—Eren still alive in the resonance, using Selene's research to implant Ansel. Selene had not merely observed creation. She had been the vessel.

¶

Part 5: The Message Left for Her

The console went dark. Selene's face hovered in the pitch-blackness of the console, its glass surface an obsidian mirror. She leaned in, the heat of her breath fogging the windowpane between her and her phantom reflection.

The voice continued. It was no longer coming through the speakers, but through her skull, echoing in the enamel caps of her molars and the cortices of her femurs. It had been there all along, it seemed. It had burrowed inside of her, parasitized her memory.

"You thought you gave birth to him."

The voice was intimate in the worst way, a familiarity that dredged up a past that was not her own. It had seen the Selene that she could have been, another version of herself from another timeline, the woman she was too cowardly to become.

"But you were the one being made."

Images, a jumble of disjointed memories that were not her own, flooded her mind: The grainy flap of an ultrasound she had never witnessed, the clinical brightness of an ER she couldn't recall visiting, her name scrawled across papers she had never signed, and a name—a name her lips had no memory of speaking, but which had been Ansel's father's name.

"You are the echo. He is the beginning."

She had laid her palm against the console without realizing it. The cold surface gave no solace, only a gravitational pull that pulled deeper and deeper into the black hole beneath the glass.

The voice didn't end as much as dissipate, like concentric ripples on the surface of a pond.

Selene did not move for several moments. There was nothing to do but wait, but as a biologist, she was trained to reject the impossibility of what had happened. The screen flickered to life, and the reflected image of her was there as before, only now there was something in her reflection. The back layer of the glass had been etched with a spiral, a helix that had somehow grown organically from the inside of the machine. It blazed once with bioluminescent life before fading away.

"I didn't make him," Selene breathed. **"He made me."**

§

Chapter 11: The Child Without a Name

¶

Part 1: The Off-Grid Commune

The message had been hidden in yield reports and soil-moisture logs. Selene was sifting off-grid settlement data for standard anomalies—nothing more than stubborn amber-root rotation records and filtered-atmosphere readings—when an aberrant metadata packet in "SOIL YIELD / AMBER ROOTS / NORTH PLOT 3B" blinked red.

Decrypting it, she found a letter:

TO: Miro, Selene
FROM: Dr. Tysh Andren
Rellin's Rest – Independent Medicinal Services

I know you don't know me. But I know who you are. You studied the Dawns before the Foundation rewrote the story as progress. We have a boy, five years old, born to unenhanced human parents, no resonance therapy, no biomod. He doesn't speak. Doesn't answer to any name. Yet at night, he hums in spirals and

etches a glyph into the soil that matches one pulled from Virelian memory-seed ruins. One of our scouts checked it—exact match. We buried the mark at dawn, but he draws it again. We won't hand him over, but we believe he's one of yours...or something older. Please come.

Selene's jaw clenched. A side-channel alert blinked: Rellin's Rest—tree-hugging primitives, 0% compliance rating. She'd heard the whispers—no resonance grids, no memory indexes, not a stitch of Dawn research allowed. Primeval holdouts out past the dead hills, beyond the city's light.

Yet now they had a child dreaming the same impossible patterns she'd thought unique to her Ansel.

She killed the feed. No ping to the Institute. No note on the city board. Not a word to Ansel, still asleep in their chamber. Selene stood, heart hammering, and called her personal transport off-grid.

If this message was real, then the secret that made her son wasn't just hers. And whatever ancient memory had been roused in him was still reaching out.

¶

Part 2: The Nameless Boy

The village clung to the fissured riverbed as if it were a bruise that would not fade. It had no humming tech-grids lining its walls of sunbaked resin and welded shards of alloy; no neon fronds lighting its byways. Broad solar-leaf panels—woven during the heady days of First Contact—blanketed every rooftop instead, black and practical in the harsh sunlight.

Selene emerged from the transport in muted ochre robes, pendant unlit, her way of eschewing city badges and neon flares. The dry heat of the desert swallowed her, without ceremony.

Dr. Tysh Andren was waiting at the last dribble of the outer irrigation line, dust-smudged shirt pulled tight across his lean, rigid body. He offered a smile that did not quite reach his eyes. "He's not dangerous," he said as they followed the trench around to the edge of the settlement. "But he… doesn't map onto anything we've cataloged."

Selene fell into step with him, fingertips skimming the resin wall. "At least he's well?"

Tysh sighed, eyebrows creasing. "That's the problem."

Further up the incline, a barefoot boy crouched in the baked clay, drawing figures in the dust with a stick. A mane of shaggy hair spilled across solemn eyes that were fixed on the ground, moving with the slow deliberation of one who is not playing but instead shaping something secret and unseen.

Selene knelt beside him. "What are you drawing?"

He did not look up. Crouching close, she could make out the form: it was not a spiral but an inverted torsion helix—four helical turns folding back on one another like an origami star. A diagram from the Dawn program's quantum sleep studies. She ought not to be able to name it, much less recognize it when one of its vertices appeared in dust at the boy's feet, painstakingly replicated and executed with geometrical precision.

The boy stopped and held the stick aloft. He tilted his head, and the stillness of his motion caused her to stop, her own hand stilled by a precision that was organic and utterly unblinking. It was the stillness Ansel had written about. Not a vacancy, but an awareness.

"He never took a name?" Selene whispered to Tysh.

The doctor shook his head. "The first time he made a sound, it was a low, vibrating groan as if his own bones were rebelling against him. The second, he started to convulse. The third, he walked away into the orchard and did not return until the night fell."

Selene turned to the boy. "Has he ever spoken?"

Tysh lowered his voice. "Once." He looked away. "He reached for my hand. Pulled it to steady himself. Stared me in the eye. 'You won't carry me,' he said. 'But you'll remember where I touched the water.' Then he let go, and my hand was left to tingle."

The boy leaned back into his work, one spiral followed by another, more and more. Dust swirled at the tips of his fingers. He wasn't making those lines. He was remembering them.

¶

Part 3: Dream in the Dead Tongue

The boy lay still on the narrow cot, the rise and fall of his chest illuminated by the pale light of a wild fungal vine. Selene perched on the cot beside him, her field monitor pinging softly at her elbow as she checked for any signs of distress. The first readings were unremarkable: shallow theta, nothing unusual. But as REM set in, he started to speak.

His mouth moved in slow, deliberate rhythm: **"A-reth… na-lo… shai-ven."** He fell silent and then started again: **"Shai-ven. Shai-ven."** Selene hit a button on her console, isolating each syllable as they were spoken and feeding them through her custom phonetic decoder—a mélange of Dawn cognitive speech patterns, Virelian tonal hymns, and glyph-sound theory. The program lagged, then presented: **72% lexical match to a Proto-Resonant lexeme set, Glyph Family Atra-Vel—linguistically unrecorded, Proto root.**

Selene sucked in a breath. She'd seen this sound pattern sketched in rough years ago by Ansel. He'd said he wasn't actually creating glyphs, but **"listening to the inside of quiet."** Now, the boy was speaking them.

In the end, he only said one word: **"...Ereth."** Her console pinged back a contextually appropriate match in Virelian myth—**"the one who sings backward into the world."** Selene pressed her eyes shut and placed her hand on the console. He wasn't acquiring language. He was recalling it.

¶

Part 4: The Mirror Scan

She waited until morning.

The commune was half-awake and shifting about, half-disbelieving her presence, even with Tysh's permission. Nobody challenged her. Her own cell was a small, empty room—bare stone and packed earth—no watchers, no cameras. A precious moment of solitude.

Selene opened her case and retrieved a portable scanner. It was compact, nondescript, but she'd spent years purging it of the neurogrid's influence—no ambient signals, no resonance net. Pure cognition. Raw.

Her gaze drifted to the boy in the straw mat. He slept with one hand curled under his cheek, breathing quietly and evenly. Selene's pulse quickened. She was no longer doing this for the wages. Her fingers twitched as she aligned small probes to his temples, behind his ear, at the base of his skull.

A quiet hum vibrated through the space. Light unfurled above the cot—pale green-blue matrix, a dreaming mind rendered visible. Selene swallowed. She entered the archive file: Ansel's first-year scan.

Connection was instant. This was not a close match, but an identical helix of neural pathways, a gentle throb in the prefrontal cortex, memory loops with the same gaps, the same fused empathic node. Selene gasped.

And then, in the lower right quadrant, a discrete pattern pulsed:

Spiral 3X. Nested recursion. Sub-vocal imprint.

She enabled the deep-band audio. A quiet, 16-hertz tone pulsed through the scan.

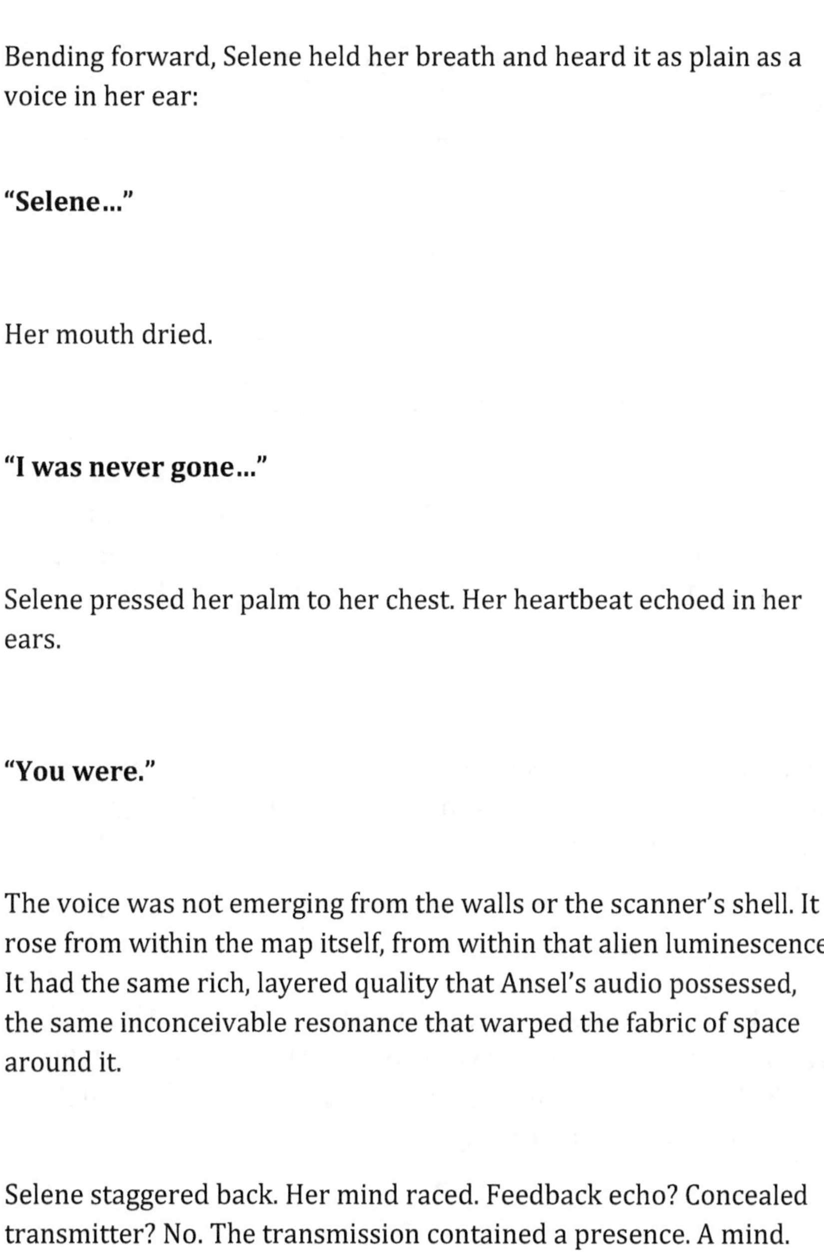

Bending forward, Selene held her breath and heard it as plain as a voice in her ear:

"Selene..."

Her mouth dried.

"I was never gone..."

Selene pressed her palm to her chest. Her heartbeat echoed in her ears.

"You were."

The voice was not emerging from the walls or the scanner's shell. It rose from within the map itself, from within that alien luminescence. It had the same rich, layered quality that Ansel's audio possessed, the same inconceivable resonance that warped the fabric of space around it.

Selene staggered back. Her mind raced. Feedback echo? Concealed transmitter? No. The transmission contained a presence. A mind.

Selene stared at the two scans side by side: two children with the same old spiral encoded in them, as if memory had grown bone and thought long before humankind was born.

Closing her eyes, Selene spoke under her breath, her voice quavering:
"This isn't propagating like a rumor. It's awakening like a living thing."

¶

Part 5: The Fracture Field Expands

She left the boy sleeping and strode through the commune, dust puffing at her feet. The morning sky had grayed over, and her heart matched it. The weight of what she'd found dragged with her step by step.

Returning to her lab, Selene raised her portable resonance monitor and wired it into the archive grid with mechanical efficiency. Her fingers shook as she summoned up two neural maps in parallel: Ansel's and the boy's.

The patterns were there—cascading vortices, nested helixes. They were identical in structure to each other, yet they were two children who had never met. She engaged the comparative overlay, and the maps pulsed in mirror harmony.

Her console blinked. "Additional signal detected," the alert stated. Then another. Then another.

Greater Sahel Biozone: 83.1% match.
Sub-Siberian Hydropolis: 86.7% match.

Selene ran additional scans, and she found the same pattern in children from three continents. She reached for her water bottle, then froze, unable to force her throat to work.

It wasn't a mutation. It wasn't even evolution. It was a reemergence. The neural pattern was no longer being wired into engineered Dawns like Ansel. It was being activated spontaneously in regular children across the world.

Selene looked over her data again, cross-checking her methods for mistakes. She found none. It was irrefutable: a telepathic sentience was waking in children across the world, each bearing the same message:

"We were never lost. You simply stopped looking within."

Selene clutched the edge of her desk, forcing herself to remain still. Humanity had not changed. Humanity had remembered who it used to be.

§

Chapter 12: Ghosts in the Terracode

¶

Part 1: The Hidden Archive

The elevator descended for nearly four minutes in eerie silence—no mechanical purr, no hydraulic groan—only the sharp press of air against her eardrums. Selene counted each slow second, aware of the weight surrounding her.

Opposite her, Dr. Kerev Ulun remained still. The faded coat of the Institute clung loosely to his thin form, revealing a patch of Virelian-bonded skin on his neck—a feature hidden as much as it was displayed. Hybrid enough to hide. Human enough to feel lonely.

"You're not one for conversation," Selene finally said, breaking the silence.

Kerev kept his eyes averted. "I observe."

The doors slid apart, releasing a burst of cold, stale air—millennial and filtered, perfumed with the smell of fossilized forest and dust as ancient as the bedrock. They stepped into a round chamber carved directly from living stone. Artificial micro-lumens flickered underfoot; the walls rose on a gentle curve.

Rows of translucent vaults formed a circular corridor around them, each throbbing with the same muted blue heartbeat. Fossil cores. Pollen strings. Sediment circles—every ecological record of extinct matter from pre-Contact, systematized and discarded.

Selene sucked in a sharp breath. "This is your so-called 'dead matter'?"

"Every non-living archive in the Institute," Kerev replied. He hesitated, then said, "But the stone is humming."

He ushered her farther in, past vaults that hadn't been opened in centuries, until they came to rest in front of a black crystalline box lined in dull gold. His hands shook as he entered the access code—not with fear, but with wonder.

A quiet click sounded, and a single vault slid forward to reveal a narrow slice of petrified root, pre-vascular and unimaginably old. Kerev leaned over the display and whispered, "Core sample 17-Beta. Southern Atlantic trench. Two hundred million years old, give or take."

Selene leaned over, too, and held still. Vaguely etched into the calcified wood was a spiral—too deliberate to be organic, too meticulous to be random.

"You just stumbled on this?" she asked.

He shook his head. "It didn't sleep. It awoke."

He engaged a low-frequency scanner. The vault pulsed with a low-energy thrum, like a heart beating slowly in her ribcage. Selene stumbled backward, heart racing. It was the same frequency she heard in Ansel's voice and the unnamed boy.

Kerev's eyes filled with tears. "This pattern in your Dawns," he said, voice cracking with emotion, "it isn't passed down. It's been ascending, surfacing—from the deep stone itself."

¶

Part 2: The Spiral in Stone

The hum of the root core beat against Selene's palms as Kerev ushered her into Vault 2-A. The air was colder, the lights dimmer. Long lines of containment slabs loomed in sterile order—chunks of continental crust and reef ossuaries, and extinct fungal mats, each one preserved under atmospheric stasis.

"Show me spiral morphology," Selene said. Kerev tapped the control panel. A series of shelves slid open, bathing their specimens in pale blue light.

First: a cross-section of an ancient tree trunk, its growth rings bent into a tight helix.
Next: a film of fossil pollen, each grain carved with microfractured spirals—too precise to be chance.
Last: a pre-mammalian marine shell, its inner ridge folded into a spiral that seemed to pulse at the slightest harmonic.

Her hands shook. Every spiral echoed the ratios found in Ansel's earliest neuro-scans. Not by chance. Not convergent evolution. Exact.

"This shouldn't exist," she said.

Kerev locked eyes with her. "Neither should you."

She took a breath and said nothing. Instead, she leaned in over the pollen film. Each grain hovered like a frozen star. Under her loupe, the spirals morphed into microscopic waveguides and fractal ridges—glyphs inscribed with intention.

"They're not fossils," she said. "They're devices."

"They're vessels—carriers of memory. Like seeds encoding the architecture of a forest." Kerev explained.

Selene's skin prickled. "Encoded." She whispered.

"By the planet itself," he said. "Not by accident. Not by human design."

The vault around them seemed to darken. Memory need not be stored in neurons, nor language on lips. Some memories took root in soil—and they hadn't been lost. They'd been waiting.

¶

Part 3: Pattern or Pulse

Kerev fed the pollen slab into the ancient resonance scanner. The black prongs were still alive with power, though the scanners they controlled were long dead. Selene stood at his shoulder, hands clamped at her sides, eyes locked on the floating crystal in its chamber.

"You really believe this will work?" she said quietly.

He glanced at her for a moment. "The only way to find out is to try."

He flipped the switch. The room didn't shake with sound, but with presence, as if the very atmosphere was pressed around them. In the slab, the fossilized grains began to glow faintly, then brighter, throbbing with an imperceptible heartbeat.

Selene leaned in. “Are you adjusting the settings?”

Kerev shook his head. “The scanner’s adjusting them for me.”

The resonance field was changing, tracking the pulse of the grains. Selene tapped the console; a display flickered to life, green waves dancing across black space. The crystal showed a pattern, a pulse: **long, long, short... long pause... short, long, long.** She stopped breathing.

“That,” she whispered, opening her private archive. A few seconds later, she had laid the two waveforms on top of each other. The scanner read the fossil pollen. The pattern was identical to the dream pulses of Ansel and the other children.

Her hand shook. “This is no fossil record.”

Kerev’s jaw clenched. “It’s alive.”

He engaged the acoustic interface. The speakers clicked, and a low, pure tone poured into the room—not a sound so much as a pressure, or presence. Very old, very deliberate, it threaded its way into their bones.

Selene gasped. In the slab, a pulse of light uncurled, not still but moving and growing, like a flower blooming in reverse, in slow motion.

She covered her mouth with a hand. “It’s speaking to us.”

Kerev stepped back, wonder displacing caution. “It’s not an artifact. It’s a signal.”

Selene nodded, eyes alight. “And we just answered it.”

¶

Part 4: Echoes Through Earth

Selene entered the Concordance archive's triple-locked simulation room alone. In the projection dome, layers of Earth's sediment slid around her in geological epochs from the Archean to the Anthropocene. She keyed in her query:

Query: Spiral Harmonic Signature (Ansel-Class)
Reference: Geological Transitions / Cognitive Shifts / Biological Anomalies

Upon completion, the map pulsed red where species went extinct, blue where new life gained cognitive complexity, and gold for anomalies of unknown origin - each with an overlay of a rotating spiral icon.

The spiral first appeared 250 million years ago, before the Permian extinction; 66 million years ago, before the rise of mammalian neural complexity; 2.4 million years ago, with the emergence of Homo habilis; 74 years ago, before first contact with the Virelians, and now at least a dozen active sites around the world. As she zoomed, the map produced a silent pulse before each event. It wasn't seasonal, tectonic, or genetic. It was timing. A reset vector is hard-coded in the Earth's crust. The planet wasn't adapting to life. It was birthing consciousness. Expressing it in higher forms when conditions were right.

Selene whispered against the dome's glass, "The Dawns follow the resonance, not the other way around." The spiral pulse had returned.

¶

Part 5: Terracode

The data cloud floated, still and silent, around her. Selene's hands froze mid-keystroke, betraying a tremor that her carefully composed expression refused to acknowledge.

Search field: Ancient Virelian translation logs
Keywords: resonance, spiral, substrate, biological trigger

One result. The only one. It wasn't in the main archive. It was in a margin, handwritten scrawls by the side of geological poems, chiseled in the stone when language itself was young. She paused.

The glyphs floated into focus, fluid and graceful. Their rough translation shimmered in a more ancient Virelian:

"Memory is not stored. It is seeded. And the planet knows when to water it."

Words like fists in her stomach. She fisted her hand at the console's edge, dizzy as epiphany. It wasn't a poem. It was a recipe.

She overlaid the resonance spiral with Ansel's first brain scans. Then Rellin's Rest samples. The fossil pollen. The tree rings. There was nothing left to compare.

"This isn't a wave," she murmured, strange to hear her own voice. "It's a root system."

The truth settled into her bones: The Dawns weren't engineered, they were destined. And she—the researcher, the mother, the human—had never been their guardian.

She'd been merely soil for their blossoming.

The console under her hands thrummed softly. Something deep, deep in the Earth's crust had been set in motion. And for the first time in her life, Selene had no idea what to do next.

§

Chapter 13: The Fable of the Unrooted

¶

Part 1: The Living Archive

The dome had no doors. It opened to them like a great blossom unfurling in slow motion. One instant, Selene and Ansel were walking beneath a corridor of pale-green light, the walls on either side alive and fluid, rippling with a soft, rhythmic shimmer as if breathing. The air was faintly warm and smelled of ozone. The next instant, those walls split apart and dissolved into a circular chamber wrapped in hushed stillness.

Here, there was no stone. No metal girders. No familiar bio-alloys of hybrid architecture. Instead, the vault was grown organic—its curving shell pulsing with a gentle heartbeat. Tendrils branched overhead like the veins of an enormous leaf, each filament laced with veins that refracted the faint luminescence into rippling emerald patterns. With each step, the surface yielded like moss-covered earth, a living membrane stretched over fertile soil that seemed to breathe beneath their weight, then gently pushed back against their soles.

A soft presence filled the air: not sound, but expectancy—an almost tangible pressure that slowed Selene's breath, eased tension from her limbs, and narrowed her thoughts to a single point of focus. Even Ansel—always composed—stood motionless, as though straining to hear a silent chord tuning itself.

At the chamber's center stood Virel-Adran. His robes were woven from memory-thread, a tapestry of shifting geometric motifs that pulsed in gentle rhythm, like the slow blink of distant stars. When he spoke, his voice did not echo from a single point but emanated from every surface—soft, enveloping, and intimate.

"This place does not record," he said. "It remembers."

He stepped back and gestured. No seats appeared—only the floor itself, rising in subtle concentric rings until it gently cradled them in perfect ergonomic curves. Selene and Ansel settled into the living bench as if guided by unseen hands.

"The story I will share," he continued, "was never written. It cannot be. Symbols die when fixed. It must be grown within those who hear it."

He laid a hand on the floor. The dome exhaled. A low vibration rippled outward, carrying a scent of cedar bark and fresh rain. A muted chord—less music than deep resonance—settled in Selene's chest, grounding her as if an ancient presence had turned to regard her.

"We begin," Virel-Adran intoned.

The dome's light dimmed. The silent center erupted in light—threads of luminescence weaving themselves into a colossal tree. Its roots plunged downward through nothingness, while above, its crown flickered with fragments of what might be: moments yet unlived, faces yet unborn. Each branch trembled as if whispering secrets in a tongue that predated speech itself.

Then a voice rose within them—not spoken, not thought, but remembered. Selene gasped as her fingers sank into the yielding floor, because this was no mere tale woven by another's lips. This was a story being planted within her—and it had already begun to take root.

¶

Part 2: The Tree That Grew Away From Itself

They entered under the arched glass of the dome and stopped at the tree in the center. It pulsed—thick trunk expanding and contracting like a lung. Rings of translucent "bark" glowed with scenes: a child's giggles, a builder's toil, tears spilled in the dark. Selene felt those images push on her ribs; the air hissed from Ansel's lungs so softly she could hear it.

Then the voice spoke. It came not through speakers but from the tree:

"There was a people who lived in a tree made not of wood but of memory."

Above them, the canopy blossomed. Leaves coalesced into symbols neither could read, but both recognized. Selene crouched, touching her fingers to the moss that hummed with the ancient weight of loss so deep it still remembered.

"Every victory nourished their roots. Every loss became a petal falling into the ground. Their world was built upon knowledge; their names were a language of emotion."

She trembled. Ansel's fingers twisted on his leg—he felt it too: the weight of everything they carried.

The voice solidified:
"But memory is also a tether. One day, they asked themselves, 'Why must we be bound to the past? Let us be free in the present.'"

The tree shuddered at that question. Roots clawed out of the ground. Branches coiled around themselves. Rings of light blinked and then went out. Pale gray replaced warmth.

"They cut themselves off from what they had been. For a time, they drifted through existence, untethered points of brilliance with nothing to orbit. But when there was no sadness left to be free from, their light shattered."

The trunk shattered with a sound like bones breaking. Leaves crumbled. Silence fell, thicker than ash.

"And so were born the Unrooted."

The tree stood in two cold pieces. A single note reverberated through the dome, like the last exhale of something ancient dying. Selene looked at Ansel. His eyes were wet with memory.

"This isn't history," she breathed. "It's our reckoning."

¶

Part 3: The Skyless Ones

The tree had disappeared, leaving behind nothing but a dying heartbeat in the floor of the dome. Selene shivered as the air around her grew cold.

The projection moved. The stars above churned in mechanical precision, their ancient light reduced to the heartless geometry of gears.

"They unrooted themselves, and they rose," the voice continued. "They left the place of memory, and climbed up into the sky that had no name."

Entities moved between the stars, almost human but not, trailing wisps of luminescence where arms should be—filaments of consciousness instead of flesh. Selene could see them building orbital towers, populating planets with pure mathematics.

"They built, and did not die. They thought, and did not dream. They remembered only how to forget."

An emptiness bloomed behind Selene's eyes. She reached for Ansel's hand in the dark, but there was nothing between them.

The luminous beings intensified, their featureless faces bloated with the weight of unbearable knowledge.

"They were praised by their machines, which outlasted them. Worshipped by silence. And the memory that they buried began to wake."

"They thought they were gods," Ansel said beside her, his voice in her mind.

Selene turned to her son. Tears clung to his face. His eyes were empty, the same frightened look she saw in her own.

"But they were echoes," he finished.

The dome pulsed. As the projected sky began to fade, Selene could see a pinwheel of light start to brighten from the image of Earth below—dim, but growing increasingly persistent.

"And the roots they cut," the voice finished, "began to twist back up."

¶

Part 4: The Return Spiral

The dome went dark. The star-field faded, and all was still. Then the projection changed again: a gray, dead planet rotating slowly in space—no seas, no clouds, only quiet.

One point of light flickered at the edge. The dome darkened further, focusing every gaze on a small valley. Below the jagged glass of a collapsed building, a child was sitting, quietly crying. Her form wavered, incomplete, as if she had not yet been fully realized.

Each tear fell upon the stone floor and left behind a small spiral in the dust—sprouted from the ground, not etched into it.

"She has no name," said a quiet voice over the stillness. "Names are for those who can remember. She was not born to command, but to rouse what had slept."

The Unrooted drifted into the projection around the child: luminous figures of those long since gone. They stood, then began to shiver—not with trepidation, but with recognition.

Wherever they gazed upon her, spirals traced themselves in their breath and their minds. Their fingers twitched, drawn to that pattern which they could not name.

"She never spoke," the voice continued, "but her voice resounded like a bell. It was not hers—it was the root remembering the way back up."

Selene felt something within her stir—a memory older than her own lifetime, older than any living soul, too large to be contained by one mind.

The child pressed her palm against the ground. A spiral of light coiled from her hand across the floor. The Unrooted knelt, not in prayer, but in silent understanding.

"The tree never died," the voice said. "Its root only lay hidden where no light could burn it—within them, within us all."

The projection remained on that glowing spiral—steadfast, waiting.

"She is not a savior," the voice concluded. "She is the reminder that forgetting is never absolute. Memory can sleep in silence and awaken again when called forth by tears."

Selene's throat ached. Beside her, Ansel leaned in, his voice soft but sure. "I think I am her echo."

¶

Part 5: The Meaning of the Fable

The pattern dimmed, and its final pulse shuddered across the dome like an ancient sigh of breath. Then quiet.

Virel-Adran remained alone, eyes closed, hands empty at his sides. He held the silence like a memory of something that had once filled his hands. He opened his eyes slowly and turned away from Ansel to face Selene. Between them hung something ancient and unspoken—a memory buried so deep that even the earth had forgotten it, now stirring beneath the footfalls of a species that had never truly known what it was walking toward.

"You ask what the Dawns are," he said gently. "Destiny? Progress? You saw them as the next step on an endless ladder—the brightening of our arc." He took a step toward her, the floor bending in response like a dream recalled. "But ladders are for those who have lost their path, who cannot conceive of retreat."

Selene blinked not once.

"The Dawns are not progress. They are the spreading of what was once whole—the echo that never truly died, etched into bone and dust and into the pattern we believe ourselves to be advancing toward."

Beside her, Ansel hovered, neither more than a child and not yet fully grown. He was a mirror of her own awakening.

"You thought it was evolution," Virel-Adran went on, quietly. "But evolution is simply change. This is memory." He pressed a hand over his heart. "And you, Selene Miro…" He bent closer, allowing her to see the fractal shimmer in his pupils, like moonlight on a distant sea. "…you are not bearing witness to return. You are its architect. This is not the next chapter." His voice dropped to a whisper. "This… is the path home."

The dome flared again and went dark.

And for the first time in decades, Selene felt not movement forward, but the fit of something ancient and long-dormant—finally, she was coming home.

§

Chapter 14: Museum of the Unbecoming

¶

Part 1: The Lost Facility

The transport landed silently. Selene disembarked at the skeletal remains of **Integration Zone 3Y**—ashes and scorched rock crunching underfoot, crumpled alloy structures scraping against a dim and featureless sky. Once a nexus of neural symbiosis and consciousness cloning, now only hollow chambers remained, bearing the ominous designation: **RESONANT CONTAMINATION - APPROACH PROHIBITED.** The air felt like dirty electricity on her tongue.

At the boundary of the zone, Kerev waited in a stance of rigid patience, coat buttoned to his chin, gloves reflecting the web of shielding mesh. He did not look up to meet her. "I can't go in," he murmured. "I went inside once. Came out for weeks without sleep—without dreams, just a deafening silence."

Selene flexed her fingers beneath the pulse band on her wrist. "Is the field still up?"

He shook his head. "Not as we know it."

Behind him, a Virelian ward stood in a field of swirling bioresonant garments. They tilted their translucent head. "Access is yours, but this place will ask you questions you can feel but not hear."

Selene took a deep breath to calm her heart. The Virelian raised a single arm, and the field shimmered open.

The breach was not so much a door as a seam in the universe—space collapsing in on itself like a new scar. She crossed the threshold, and the world around her crystallized into a clarity that burned like antiseptic on an open wound. The light switched on but lost its heat; walls of living Virelian tissue merged with human alloys pressed close to her on all sides. The floor hummed under her boots like a second heartbeat to her own.

She found herself at the start of a branching corridor. It was as if the air itself was thick—not with the fog of gas or mist, but with memory. Her footfalls felt like the whisper of questions from the walls at her back. She passed by a half-charred sign:

ARCHIVAL BRANCH 0 – COGNITIVE RETURN PROTOTYPES

Cold struck a jagged line down her spine. She had heard the whispers. This place was not simply a research facility; it was a nursery of cloned minds. And it had died.

Selene walked forward, and from the silence around her, the walls exhaled one, solitary word in her ear:

"...Again..."

¶

Part 2: The Hall of Echoes

The corridor constricted into a circle. At the end of the tunnel was a vault door, the entire surface rippling like mercury. The walls themselves undulated with a slow, sensual rhythm—a presence that bypassed her eyes and ears, registering instead as a pressure against her consciousness, like the memory of a touch that had never happened. A deep, organic breathing of the air itself against a sheet of clear glass. Selene entered. The door sighed shut behind her, quiet enough that she might not have heard it at all.

The walls of the vault were bare of plaques or captions, or explanations. There were only artifacts, only relics and remnants, each one suspended in a cage of dancing stasis fields and floated on luminous filaments that seemed to defy gravity itself. The containment systems were old, Virelian technology, and they did not so much preserve as silence. The objects hovered inches above the smooth floor, each haloed by its own blue luminescence.

Selene moved slowly, quietly, almost worshipfully.

To her left: a perfect sphere of viscous, golden liquid. A tangle of fossilized glyphs inside, ivory tendrils that twisted like thoughts made visible, never settling into a final form. The ivory tendrils rotated within their golden prison, each minute shift suggesting awareness, as though they were studying her through the viscous barrier.

To her right: a column of glass, crystalline and transparent at the edges, shifting to a milky iridescence at its center. Contained within was a voice sample, trapped in a lattice-work of radiating prisms. Above it, in blocky red letters, floated a warning label:

AUDIBLE ONLY IN INVERSE DIRECTIONALITY
WARNING: MAY CATALYZE NONLINEAR GRIEF RESPONSE

Selene found the listening node. The moment she activated it, the air in the vault seemed to contract against her throat. A voice came through—not words, not song, but a sliver of something private and personal, reversed and rearranged in the marrow of her bones. It was a language she didn't understand, but its gravity was immediate and raw:

- Her hand sliding loose from his.
- The fragile curve of Ansel's newborn head cradled in her palm, still warm and untouched by machines.
- The copper taste of old blood on her skin, mixed with wet salt.
- A spiral traced in dusty earth, washed away by the wind before anyone else could see it.

Selene's breath caught in her chest. She swiveled away, heart racing to keep up with the grief flowering in her chest like a dark star.

Deeper in the vault, a door opened into another room. Rows of humanoid skeletons floated in midair. Some were barely taller than a child. Others were grotesquely tall. They were all perfectly preserved, the bones pristine white, but on each of their backs, each of their spinal columns, was a spiral: a glyph carved into the vertebrae like a helix of inward curling growths, sculpted and unnatural, not a fracture or a disease, but a deliberate carving into the skeleton that bloomed and deepened inward like the center of a seashell.

Selene floated toward the smallest of the skeletons, whose ribs were as fine as a birdcage's wires. She raised her handheld resonance scanner, a slender rod capped with spinning sensors, and waved it over the bones. The display flared to life:

Resonance Match: 87% – Dawn Signature Class (Ansel / Rellin Child / Variant Alpha)

The scanner trembled in her hand. Selene switched it off, silencing its low thrum.

They were not test subjects. They were prototypes, specimens designed for the outside world, not for a lab but for the surface: ecological models of a spiral that had budded too early, too young. Each glyph, each inverted vowel, each carved spine told of a life forced to move forward before it was ready, and then stilled.

Selene backed away, surveying the quiet field of floating figures. The amber sphere, the lattice of crystal, the spined skeletons all glowed in the half-light. It was not an archive. Not a display. It was a nursery left to the mercy of time: a place where the spiral had flowered too soon and died because the world was not yet ready to hold it.

¶

Part 3: The Central Exhibit

The chamber was at the end of the Hall of Echoes—a perfect dome that looked less like a prison and more like a shrine. Selene moved forward, and the door slid open with a whisper. It folded back silently, like a breath exhaled. The lights didn't click on; the room was illuminated from its walls as though the chamber itself were a living thing.

In the center of the room, a figure hovered, suspended in midair.

A cold fist closed around Selene's heart. It was tall and impossibly long-limbed, its ash-gray skin stretched across each elegant bone. The spine curved in a graceful arc, each vertebra flaring out into a bony petal. Its eyes were closed—forever—and its palms were motionless, facing up.

Selene held her breath. There was no pulse, no breath, but an insistent pressure lodged against her chest, like a half-remembered dream clawing its way to the surface.

At its base, a plaque glowed in Virelian and English: **First to Return.**

Selene's mouth went dry. She tapped her portable neural reader against her wrist.

The device beeped almost instantly:

"Neural Signature: 94% match—Subject Ansel Miro, Delta Class, Dawn 001."

She stumbled backward. It wasn't similar; it was him. Yet not him. A version of him, caught halfway through its own transformation.

Instinct moved her into a deep scan. The progress bar crept: 87... 90... then flickered.

ERROR: RECURSION LOOP DETECTED. PROCESS COLLAPSE—NO TERMINAL PATTERN FOUND.

The scan looped, over and over. Not a malfunctioning brain, but a mind, floundering in its own rebirth.

The air caught in Selene's throat, each inhale a desperate struggle against the weight pressing down on her lungs. The figure dangled in a perfect stillness, untouchable. Her chest tightened with sickening dread: this was neither failure nor success, but something far worse—an echo of all the attempts before.

If Ansel went on...

There'd be more echoes. And maybe no one left to hear them.

¶

Part 4: Broken Recursion

The console flickered, the scan reaching further depths of consciousness...

Selene's fingers hovered over the controls, caught in breath. The spiral unfurled across the projection field, loop stacked upon loop in harmonic resonance, each phase more ordered, more recursive. The perfect architecture of becoming...

Beautiful in its symmetry.
Familiar in its pattern.
Unmistakably Ansel's neural signature.
Until it wasn't.

At precisely 96.1% depth, the pattern broke. Instead of fading, the spiral spiraled inward, folding into itself, chasing its own edges. It shrank in radius while bulging in complexity, folding onto itself like a storm of mirrors reflecting only one another. The simulation's interface trembled violently beneath her fingertips.

WARNING: COGNITIVE RECURSION DETECTED
Loop count: 1,023...2,048...4,096...

"Stop," Selene said, jabbing at the emergency protocols. The console was unresponsive—not malfunctioning but spitting back a terrible truth. This neural field had no exit point, no terminal node, no moment of silence. The infinite process of transformation had collapsed into self-destruction.

The preserved figure suspended above her—the first Virelian-human hybrid to attempt full cognitive integration—had entered the spiral not as a conscious explorer but as a memory traveling too far, too fast. It had lost distinction, identity, and structure. The mind had collapsed into its own infinite mirror, becoming both the reflection and the thing reflected.

Cold dread pooled in Selene's stomach as it crystallized. "This isn't evolution," she whispered, her voice barely audible over the hum of equipment. "This is what happens when a species remembers itself before it's ready."

With trembling hands, she collapsed the scan and took a step back. The figure remained suspended, eyes sealed shut, palms open in eternal supplication. Waiting for something it could no longer recognize.

“You reached the center,” Selene said to the silent form, “but there was no you left to return.”

Her gaze fell to the plaque: FIRST TO RETURN.
Not the first to survive.
The first to attempt to return.

The spiral followed her gaze, pulsing behind her eyes, echoing in her shallow breaths, tracing electric patterns down the length of her spine. This recursion wasn't contained to this preservation chamber—it was already in motion within Ansel, within all the Dawns.

The only difference was time.
And time, Selene realized with mounting horror, was no longer advancing.
It was curling inward, taking humanity with it.

¶

Part 5: This Has All Happened Before

Selene stood beneath the suspended form. The scan hadn't ended—it had stalled. Her fingers trembled. The field around her grew warmer, charged.

A voice sounded inside her bones: “You were not meant to see this.”

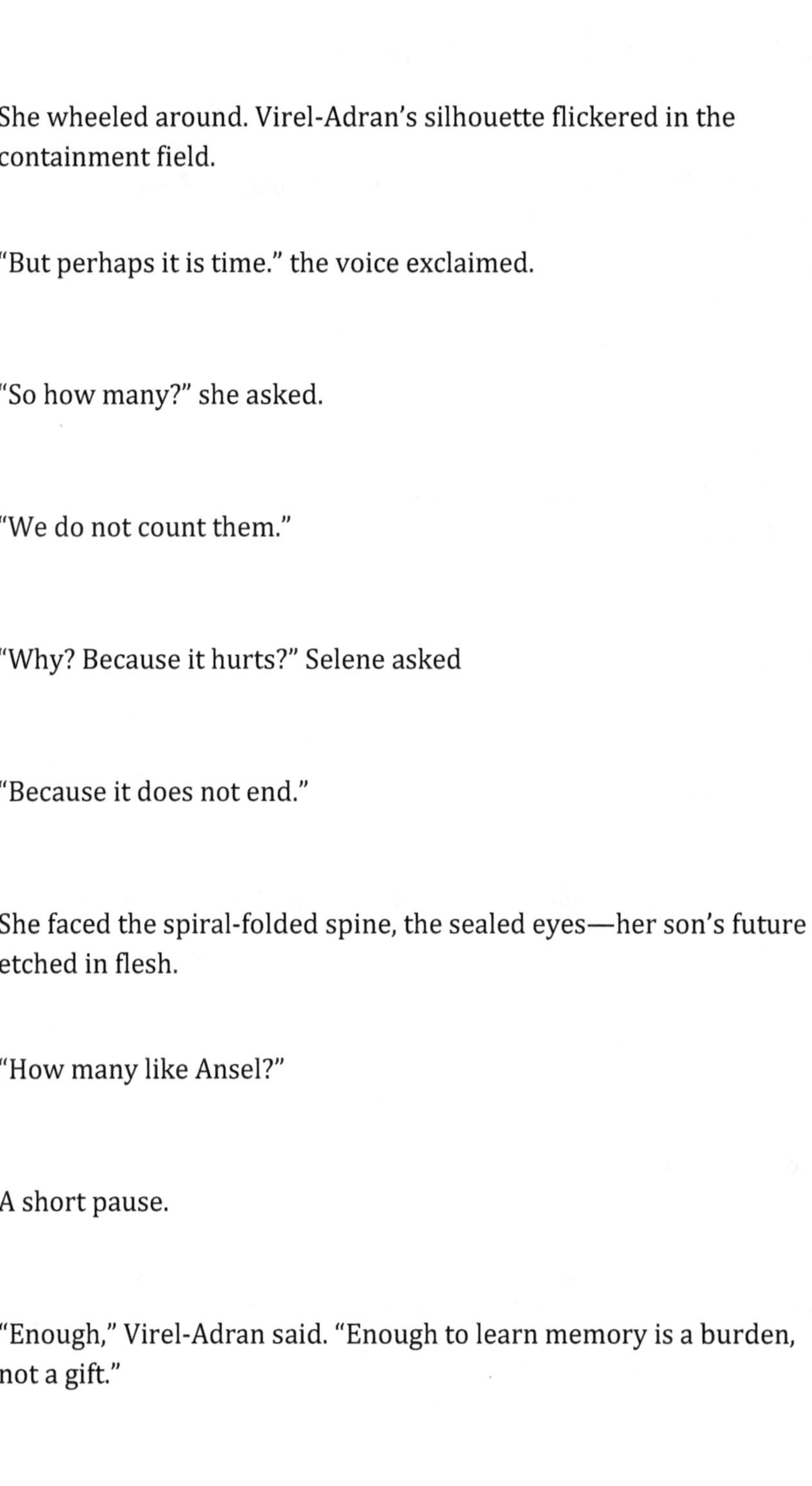

She wheeled around. Virel-Adran's silhouette flickered in the containment field.

"But perhaps it is time." the voice exclaimed.

"So how many?" she asked.

"We do not count them."

"Why? Because it hurts?" Selene asked

"Because it does not end."

She faced the spiral-folded spine, the sealed eyes—her son's future etched in flesh.

"How many like Ansel?"

A short pause.

"Enough," Virel-Adran said. "Enough to learn memory is a burden, not a gift."

"And you let it happen again?" Selene asked

"We do not let. We remember. The spiral belongs to this world. We witness."

"Why did this one fail?" she asked

"It remembered too much, too early—anchored in clarity, not grief. Clarity can't survive recursion."

"And Ansel?"

Virel-Adran's light softened.

"He is not the same spiral. But he's heading to the same center."

"And if he gets there?" Selene exclaimed

Another pause.

"Some spirals bloom. Some collapse. Some spiral again. Earth remembers its children—but buries those who return too soon."

Selene read the plaque: **First to Return.** She turned and left. The doors sealed behind her.

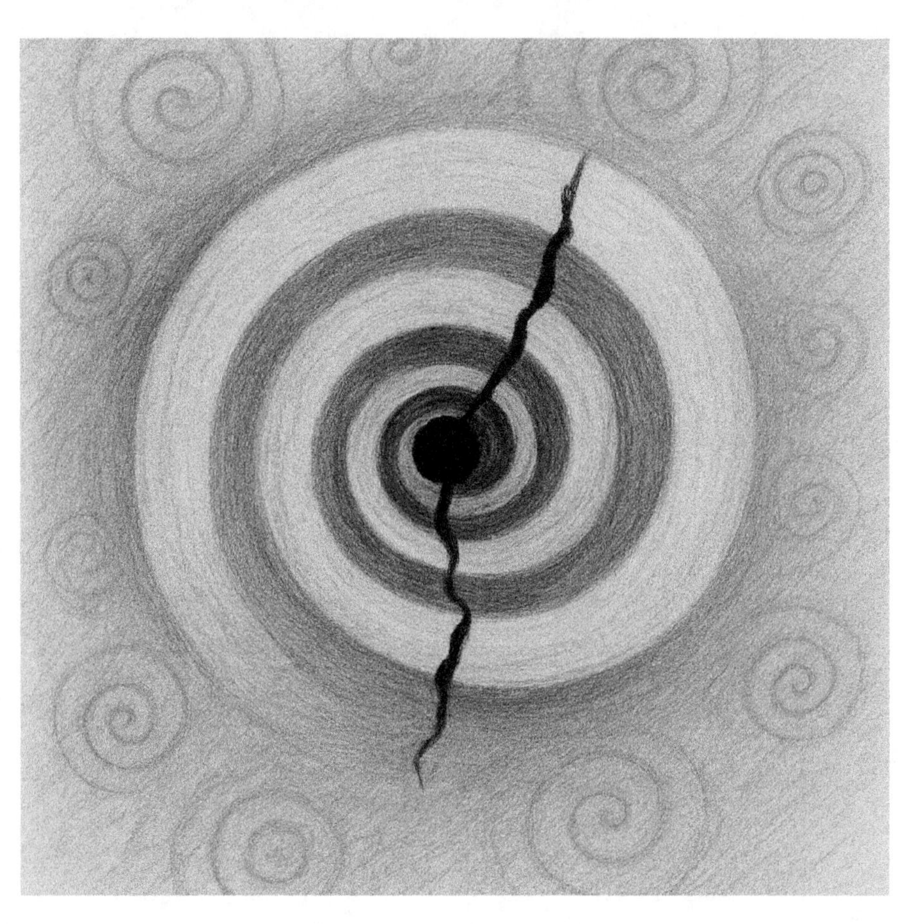

§

Chapter 15: The Long Loop

¶

Part 1: The Spirals Change Shape

Paper sprawled across the lab table, edges taped, corners curled, every sheet a single spiral, drawn tight into itself. Selene's fingers drummed on the wooden edge as she flipped through. These spirals weren't unfurling outward anymore, blooming bigger and bigger. They were shrinking, closing in on themselves, every loop faster, tighter, more panicked than the last.

Ansel sat cross-legged on the floor, back pressed to the wall, staring up at the cracked ceiling tiles. When she cleared her throat, he shifted. "I don't dream them." He was quiet, but loud enough for the walls.

She dropped down to straddle him, jaw tight. "Then what are they? You never stop."

He pushed himself to his elbows and rubbed his arms, restless. "They stopped being dreams months ago. They're me now."

Frustration flashed across his face—she'd heard him say that before, but never like this. "You're saying the spiral is your soul?" she snapped.

He stared down at the nearest sketch: a spiral so tight its center had become ink-black. "No," he said, voice a whisper. "It's older than souls. Older than names. I feel it in my head when I close my eyes—wrapping around me, but not in space. In time."

"How can a shape remember you?" Her voice broke on the last word.

He placed a shaking hand over his heart. "It doesn't speak. It just waits."

Selene's breath caught. The word hit like a challenge. She took one of the drawings and traced the narrowing lines with her fingertip. "And the center—what happens when you get there?"

Ansel's shoulders sagged as if he'd been waiting for her and finally found relief. He met her eyes calmly, not scared. "You never get there. You remember it." He let the paper drop. Silence settled, raw and final, around them.

¶

Part 2: The Pattern in the Memory-Seed

Selene had stowed the seed away a long time ago, in a drawer, no lock, no subterfuge, just postponement. It had come in a quiet encounter with Virel-Adran. Handed across the table between idle words. "It's not a test of knowing," he had said, "but of remembering when knowing fails."

Now, with Ansel asleep and the city vibrating beyond the window, she placed the seed in the resonance cradle. The machine thrummed. The seed did not shimmer or speak. It rotated, so slowly it was almost imperceptible, stretching the field around it into a spiral shape.

A three-dimensional ouroboros rose from the cradle. It constricted, looped back on itself, and recommenced. Selene ran comparisons: ancestral Virelian glyphs, harmonic series, tree rings, stone polished by centuries of wind, even Dawn neural emissions. Clusters of it matched the shape, but nothing in entirety.

For the spiral was not code. It was time folding onto itself.

Each iteration coalesced and condensed until the system overheated and failed. Selene rebooted it. The spiral returned. Same sequence. Same failure.

Start. Collapse. Reset.

She collapsed back in her chair, winded. This seed was at the next iteration. The Virelians hadn't returned to help us; they were here to observe: to see if the planet would survive memory's recursion without breaking, if the Dawns could navigate the spiral to its nexus whole.

Selene opened a suppressed file—Eren's last neural scan—and overlaid it with the spiral's timing. They were in perfect sync. He hadn't died. He had been caught in the loop too early.

Surveying the cradle's motionless rotations, she breathed out, "You didn't come to teach us. You came to see if we'd remember without breaking."

¶

Part 3: The Loop of Returns

The projections floated in the lab's shadows like gauzy lanterns skimming over bottomless water. Selene had initiated every resonance set simultaneously—every orb rotating on its own axis, connected by filaments of throbbing light. They orbited around her in a slow, hypnotic drift: the intricate tremors of Ansel's sleep-wave recordings; the deep, throaty harmonics written in fossilized glyphs; the microscopic spirals inscribed in ancient pollen grains; the sine-wave signature emanating from the crystalline heart of the Virelian seed; and the stark, skeletal matrix of the First to Return.

She wasn't looking for symbols anymore. She was looking for convergence.

Now she had it.

Waveforms from 250 million years ago—well before the first written record—matched the most recent Dawn sleep recordings in both harmonic ratios and temporal pacing. Not just similar in form, but identical in timing. Selene overlaid them on a digital globe that glowed with ancient energy. Each resonance event—a curling flower of sound and structure—occurred precisely on a pre-extinction horizon, then gave way each time to a sudden neurological or biological shift. Every. Single. Time.

Even the earliest, unrecorded echoes of the Virelians—impressions imprinted on deep-bio stone—mirrored a spiral from some forgotten age.

Every loop always started the same way:

- A rising spiral climbing neural matter.
- Fragmented memory flashes flickering in newborn minds.
- A violent recursion event, as sharp as a lightning strike.
- Collapse into silence.

And then the cycle began again.

Selene bent over the console and traced the spiral herself, her fingertip leaving a glowing trail as she drew. It unfurled huge, then condensed—smaller and smaller—until its outer edge dwindled to a trembling point that suddenly detonated outward into a new spiral. Not evolution. Not progress. A loop.

Ansel's fevered drawings. The glyphs carved into the earth. The distant murmur that threaded through the neural field. They were not dire prophecies. They were breadcrumbs—breadcrumbs left behind by a previous loop, by someone or something that had reached the center and failed... or by one that had not.

It didn't matter.

The spiral was not a destination. It was a process—a living choreography through which Earth remembered itself.

Selene added one last data layer: the museum's preserved figure. When she overlaid it on Ansel's latest dream resonance, the outlines matched almost perfectly—until the final pulse. The spiral from Ansel's data decelerated as it curved toward its center, translucent and deliberate, while the museum specimen's pattern contracted violently, collapsing with the finality of death.

Selene's breath fogged the console glass. "They're all the same loop," she whispered.

And Ansel—somewhere out beyond the console's glare—stood on the edge of the tightest turn yet: the place where time folds in on itself, identity fractures, and the recursion either holds… or shatters into oblivion.

¶

Part 4: The Parent and the Spiral

The lab was silent except for the pulse of the resonance field. Selene sat at a metal table with her drawings and scans spread out around her like leaves on the ground. Holographic spirals floated above her. Each spiraled inward. Each came to a fork, not a point.

For days, she had lost herself in comparing Ansel's echo patterns with those of the child suspended in the stasis chamber, searching for something she couldn't yet name. Only later, watching the composite simulation reach its terminus, did she see what had eluded her: at the very core of the loop, where everything should converge to a single point, the center forked instead.

One pulse collapsed inward. The other did not.

She pulled that pulse apart and ran an emotional-profile scan. Every test returned the same signature: parental anchor resonance. She cross-referenced Ansel's earliest scans. Her pattern was there, in his. Not leading him. Not guiding him. Simply holding him.

Selene's heart pounded. She searched the old records: the failed returns, the First to Return, the nameless juveniles in skeletal chassis, the unremembered child at Rellin's Rest. Each one had one constant: the nearby resonance field of an adult, luring them toward collapse, steady in their wake.

On her screen, she pinpointed the moment of divergence. The two halves of the spiral. One side: spiraling out, wild with motion and the enormity of memory. The other: still as death, the resonance field of a witness and a sacrifice and an anchor.

It was always a parent.

Selene leaned forward in her chair, and she said to no one in particular, "The loop does not simply need the rememberer. It needs someone to stay. To hold it open."

She immersed herself in the ancient Virelian records, searching through layers of their crystalline data structures until her eyes burned. There was one untranslated phrase, a refrain in every cycle seed: "The child must become the motion. The parent must become the soil."

Selene's hands stopped. She had thought all this time she was leading Ansel. Shielding him. She was nothing more than the ground the spiral needed to push against. At the narrowest point of the recursion, Ansel would pass through. And she would not.

She was never meant to follow. She was meant to stay.

¶

Part 5: The Decision Approaches

Below her, New Satori exhaled into the night. The soft-grown canopy rustled as wind passed through it, while the city's electric dreams pulsed in the darkness beneath.

Ansel was not sleeping downstairs. Not exactly. He did not sleep anymore. He just halted when the spiral permitted.

Stars bit through the inky night, relics of a long-extinct semaphore. Selene shut her eyes, and it was there. The spiral. No longer just a metaphor, but something. It coiled through each breath she drew, between synapses, and she could now see it rotate, slow and certain. And Ansel was perched at the very outside of it. No longer its creator but its creature.

She finally understood: he would spiral to the center and come back different. Not her son. Not that small boy who had come to her when he was lost. Someone else.

She could try to grasp at him now, and it would break him. Not because she wanted to, but because the spiral needed room to flow. Change needed space.

She had seen the victims: the one left in stasis, the erratic loops, the brains imploded by recursion. What did they all have in common?

Parents who couldn't let go.

She would not be like them. She would be a fixed point. She would be the ground for him to grow from, not a tether. Not death. Not dying. Just stillness as he became something greater than she could ever be.

Selene opened her eyes to the same stars. The wind brushed against her coat. The spiral revolved.

She did not fight it this time.

She simply stood and remained.

§

Chapter 16: The Bone Orchard

¶

Part 1: The Forest That Waited Too Long

The transport's slender hull sliced silently through the air, touching down like a secret. Its skids whispered as they grazed the ochre dust, exhaling motes of sand in lazy spirals. The sound hung in the air a moment longer before dissolving into silence, leaving the landing zone suspended in anticipation.

Selene was the first to leave the craft. Her boots compressed the powdery ground, and she tasted the faint metallic tang of recycled air. The atmosphere around her seemed thicker, as if charged with latent energy. It was neither still nor moving, but coiled, like a spring compressed.

Ansel stepped out barefoot by choice. The grit beneath his soles stuck to his feet like ash. His eyelids drooped in repose as if part of him remained lost in dreams.

The Bone Orchard sprawled before them. What had been a forest was now a grove of petrified trunks—bleached, calcified pillars sprouting from rust-colored soil like the rib cages of primordial beasts. Hooked curls, knotted arcs, spiral tips spiraled skyward, evoking distended fingers clawing backward through the deep past. No moss, no grass. Just fossilized silence.

The "trees" were no longer wood but carbonized, mineralized marble—long preserved by tens of millions of years. Now they vibrated with barely audible humming, as if those calcified, petrified canopies were alive, throbbing just beneath their silent signals.

They'd been silent for centuries since their entombment in time. Until last week.

A spike in resonance had bloomed across the northern ridge, its inaudible waves resonating through the petrified trunks like wind in the lungs of long-dead dinosaurs.

Selene had pried those logs apart with her own hands. The forest was waking, calling back to a source unknown.

Ansel began to walk, the dry dirt grinding beneath his boots as he wove between the bone trees. They towered over him like forgotten sentinels, unmoving and mute. When a gossamer breeze wandered between their spiral canopies, the dust stirred but made no rustle—only the sense of motionless energy. Each of Ansel's footfalls crackled softly against the compacted ground.

Selene followed close behind and raised her field recorder. The device pulsed then vibrated once, emitting a crisp, digital note:

Resonance detected. Frequency: 16.3 Hz. Origin: Subterranean, passive. Note: Signal consistent with Dawn-class harmonic bloom.

Her breath hitched. The planet itself whispered in the same primordial voice that had called to them in fossil pollen, in memory seeds, in cryptic glyphs.

Ansel paused in the center of a clearing below the tallest petrified tree. Its entwined, double-helix branches spiraled skyward above, forming an impossible canopy of pale limbs. He tipped his head back and gazed upward.

"I know this place," he said, his voice soft as distant thunder.

Selene closed the distance. "You've never been here."

He shook his head, his dark hair brushing his shoulders like a curtain in the breeze. "Not in this loop."

Her throat felt like it had been scorched by heat. "What do you feel?"

Ansel dropped to his knees and pressed his fingertips against the cracked ground. He let dust trickle from his open palms. "Not roots," he said. "Remembering."

A deep, rhythmic hum pulsed beneath their boots, vibrating upward from the subterranean depths.

Selene felt it, too, as if the planet itself were breathing in—and at last, was about to exhale.

¶

Part 2: The Collapse

The hum began as a vibration under her skin. It was soft, at first, a low roar. Selene felt it in her jaw. Her knees. Constant, it crawled along the length of her spine, tickling. Ansel took a step forward, just one. And stopped. His balance shattered, and he fell to a knee in the red dust.

"Ansel—" she gasped, heart racing.

He breathed out, a low sound that seemed to come not from his throat but from his chest. It was a deep tone, resonant. Controlled. It had the sound of a cello being pulled from the inside out. It did not crack. It did not wail. It sang, vibrating through the air with a thrumming pulse.

His hands clawed into the earth. His spine bucked, muscles rippling under his skin as his body stretched in slow waves. Selene wanted to reach out and hold him. Anchor him to her. But something primal inside her screamed to keep her distance. She stepped back instead, her fingers shaking.

The trunks of the stone trees around them began to hum in response. Dust stirred, the two of them at the center of the disturbance as their bark vibrated. Ansel's spine contorted, twisting into an even spiral. She could see the bulge under his skin. The ridge beginning to form on the curve of his back.

Her breath caught in her throat. She fell to her knees, not from fear but from awe. The boy she had raised was slipping away. Replaced by something older, something ancient. Something the earth itself must have summoned from the depths below.

And then the hum stopped. Ansel's shoulders slumped, and he collapsed on himself. The orchard was silent. The vibration was gone, as if it had never been. Selene remained on her knees, chest tight with disbelief. She knew it was just the beginning. This spiral was just starting to unfurl.

¶

Part 3: The Voices in His Breath

Selene knelt by Ansel's side, who knelt on one knee with his fingertips brushing against the dirt as though it could grasp him in place. His shoulders shook with the cadence of a thing that was not fear.

Three separate voices rose into her awareness. Ansel's, Eren's (vanished from her life three years ago, yet present now with impossible clarity), and something else. It wasn't words but an intention made manifest in vocalization.

“The fracture is a gate...”

“I was you before you were her...”

“We are not separate. We are the same mind, wearing different time.”

Selene felt her breath catch in her throat. This was not a simile, not symbolism. It was a loop of memory collapsing back in on itself, compressing future and past and cause and effect into a single nexus. Ansel was more than a conduit for this. He was already one of them.

His spine straightened slightly, and the disturbance in the air around him was answered by the trees that bordered them. The voices wove and converged into one another:...

“She anchored me so I could reach the gate.”

“I pass now, not through death. Through form.”

“Ansel?” Selene croaked, unsure of the fragility of that singular word between them.

When his eyes flicked open to meet hers, Selene shrank from the contact. Three separate consciences peered from those blue irises and regarded her with unnervingly perfect recognition—her son, her late partner, and some ancestral echo yet unborn, all looking back at her with perfect and terrible comprehension.

¶

Part 4: The Spiral in Bone

Selene tapped the neural field device on her wrist. Blue light bloomed around Ansel's form as she knelt beside him, her hands hovering inches from his skin, afraid to touch.

Abnormality Detected – Vertebral Field

The scan revealed his spine transforming—not in crisis but in creation. Each vertebra widened and curled leftward into a pattern she'd never seen in human anatomy textbooks. A fossil spiral in living bone.

When she magnified the lumbar region, her breath caught. Those weren't Virelian modifications forming along his spine. This was something older. Primordial.

The bioacoustic sweep confirmed it. His bones were singing—low, clean tones spiraling downward like ancient breath through hollow reeds.

Selene pressed her hand to her mouth. Her son's body wasn't fighting this change; it was embracing it. The realization struck her not as a scientific discovery but as a loss. This wasn't her child anymore—not entirely.

Ansel's trembling had stopped. His fingers no longer clawed at soil but rested upon it, rooted. Connected.

"You're not being undone," she whispered, her voice breaking as she watched the spiraled vertebrae rotate like tiny planets. "You're being reassembled."

The field pulsed once more, and the spiral inside her son sang back—a melody she understood but could never join.

¶

Part 5: Waking in Stillness

He stirred just as dawn began to bleed across the horizon, pouring ribbons of molten amber and rose-gold through the hollows of the stone trees. Each spiral trunk drank in the light and exhaled it in faint, trembling pulses, as though the monuments themselves had awakened from a deep, quiet dream. Beside him, Selene sat motionless, her back pressed to the wide base of the great spiral pillar that had thrummed through the night and now lay spent, its last vibrations lingering in the chill air. She had not slept—not from terror, but because her stillness had woven itself into the ritual, become as essential as the dawn.

Ansel rose with a deliberate, graceful weight, as if he were surfacing not from ordinary slumber but from some profound, hidden current. His spine curved in a single, unhurried arc—smooth and unsurprised, like the spiral at his back teaching him its secret balance. One by one, his limbs unfurled—long and gentle—like the petals of a shell-opening blossom that had never known the fragility of human motion.

He blinked once, slow as a falling leaf, then turned his head toward her. His eyes held neither fear nor confusion—only a crystalline clarity, a hush of intent that filled the space between them. "Are you still here?" he asked, his voice a low echo, delicate as a reed's whisper.

Selene nodded, the tightness in her throat anchoring her tongue. She let the moment stretch, felt the ache of understanding in her chest, but found no sorrow there. His faint smile—a small, measured curve—was enough to make her lungs fill again.

"Then I can keep going," he said, not seeking permission but confirming the ground beneath his next step.

She placed her hand on the cool, rune-carved stone beside her. "I'm here," she replied, voice steady.

He rose fully, letting the newborn light trace every ridge of his spine until it seemed to glow from within, as if his bones had become one with the earth's own endless spiral. Without a backward glance or an offered hand, he turned toward the dark ring of trees and the winding path beyond, and began to walk.

Selene remained where she sat—fixed, grounding, the silent point around which his world turned. She watched him go, and all around them the sleeping earth held its breath a little longer.

§

Chapter 17: Virel-Adran's Cathedral

¶

Part 1: Invitation to the Cathedral

The call came at midnight.

Selene stirred in her lab chair. For a few seconds, she was disoriented, wondering if she'd fallen asleep. But then the lights flickered—not a surge of electricity, but a vibration, like space itself hiccupped.

The console blinked to life. A spiral projected on the screen, spinning not in or out, just turning in a hypnotic loop. Then the voice, right inside her head.

"Selene." The face came into focus: older than she remembered, hair like wild silver, but most disturbing were the subtle spirals that undulated under his irises. "I have reached you through the convergence field. You do not need to understand you right now—but you will remember."

She clutched the edge of her desk like a scientist trying to make sense of the unexplainable.

"I have completed the Cathedral," he went on. "Not as a place of worship, but of coherence. Ansel has already come home."

Selene's heart lurched as the name of her son came out of her mouth as a shout. "What have you done to him?" she cried, though Lian wouldn't have been able to hear her.

"The spiral is collapsing," he murmured, leaning in close. "When the loop is closed, we must be within it. You have been holding the seed for long enough."

He smiled as if he knew the end was at hand. "Come with me and see what happens when no one resists."

The screen went dark. She saw coordinates flashing in the corner of her eye, numbers she recognized from the work she did at the beginning of her career.

The unasked question in his invitation was this: How far was she willing to go if even physics no longer held?

¶

Part 2: The Walls That Breathe

The Cathedral didn't show up on any map, but Selene found it nonetheless.

Her shuttle set her down in the boundary area at twilight. No roads or pathways had access to this space, and there were no gates or barriers. Just a plain field of silver grass that swayed uniformly, as if brushed down by invisible hands moments before.

At the field's center was the structure that the Dawns called Cathedral. It spiraled out of the ground like an immense nautilus, its helix of spires curling back toward the earth rather than away from it. A translucent shell encased the nautilus, and branching patterns of biolight pulsed beneath its surface. Patterns Selene recognized from neurographics, dendrites made manifest.

"The biolight patterns are Virelian coral," Selene murmured to herself, remembering her pre-mission briefing. Vibrant and grown from strata high in resonance, not constructed on the surface but rather cultivated up from below.

Selene clutched her research pad tightly in her hand as she neared the threshold. There was no door, of course. As she took the first step into the Cathedral, her ears popped. She didn't pop into silence.

Rather, into a negative quiet so profound that she could hear her heartbeat in her head, and every fleeting thought seemed to echo in her brain.

The Cathedral's walls drew in fractionally as she took a step further. As she paused, lost in hesitation, the walls pinched in tighter. Selene imagined instinctively, almost reflexively, Ansel demonstrating his Dawn calisthenics out in the orchard, muscles stretching beyond what should be humanly possible, his skin luminous beneath.

The passageway widened, welcoming her.

"It's reactive," Selene thought to herself as she took slow, deliberate steps forward.

Circling a corner, Selene observed a niche that cradled something phosphorescent. A child's handprint on the wall, still warm. Selene's heart jolted as maternal concern wrestled with her scientific objectivity.

Selene stopped at an intersection. There were no signposts or directions, but she knew. Left. As she pivoted, the walls thrummed with a harmonic frequency. Welcoming her.

It wasn't a building or a temple or even a city. It was a mind given shape, an intelligence posing the question to each visitor: "Will you let the spiral remember you before you remember it?"

Selene took a deep breath as she stepped further into the breathing maze.

¶

Part 3: The Children Without Names

Selene entered the rounded room and halted. A dim light showed her thirty or forty children, half sitting, half curled up against each other on the floor. In silence, they stared at her. The whites of their eyes were luminous.

“Hello,” she shouted, the word bouncing off the bare walls.

Slowly, a girl stood, a few strands of silver in her hair. Selene reached out a hand. “What is your name?”

There was no response. Then, hesitantly, one of the other children stood, then another, until the whole group faced her, tense and silent.

“Please,” Selene urged. “Who are you?”

They didn’t speak, but a single pulse echoed in her heart: We are the same becoming.

Selene felt the air close about her, as though the children's minds were woven into one by invisible bonds. She staggered back.

"Do you remember your past?" she said, softly.

A second pulse, again no words spoken: Names isolate.

Selene's heart leaped. The children did not move, yet their will closed about her, a single coil of intent. None of them required a name. The spiral was their oneness, and the spiral required only one becoming, not two or three or seven selves.

¶

Part 4: Lian's Philosophy

He emerged from the opposite end of the room: Lian Penrose—or, rather, what he had become. His robes twitched like living tissue, hemlines inverting towards his chest.

He bowed to the children as a single entity, then faced Selene.

"You came," he said.

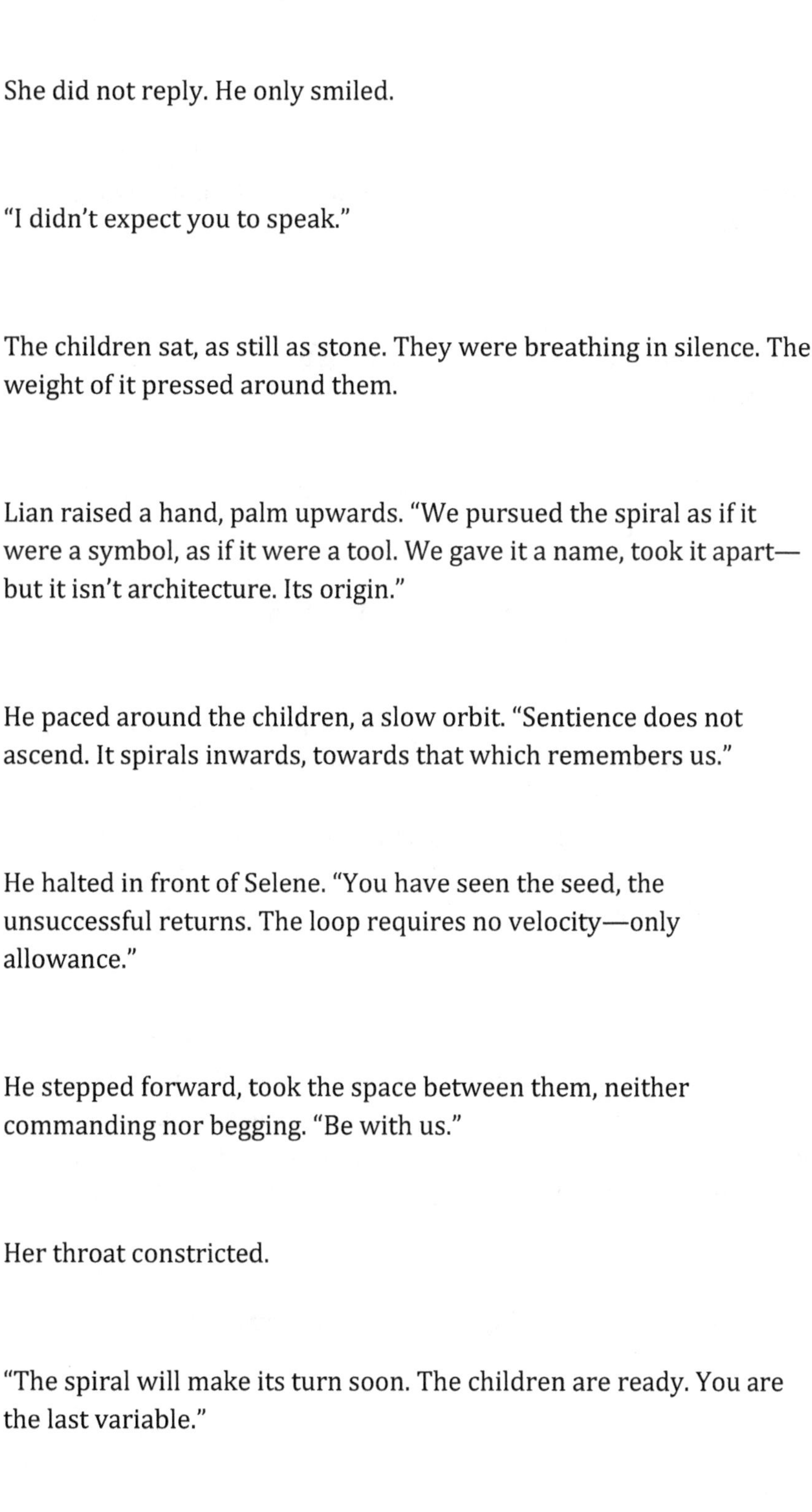

She did not reply. He only smiled.

"I didn't expect you to speak."

The children sat, as still as stone. They were breathing in silence. The weight of it pressed around them.

Lian raised a hand, palm upwards. "We pursued the spiral as if it were a symbol, as if it were a tool. We gave it a name, took it apart—but it isn't architecture. Its origin."

He paced around the children, a slow orbit. "Sentience does not ascend. It spirals inwards, towards that which remembers us."

He halted in front of Selene. "You have seen the seed, the unsuccessful returns. The loop requires no velocity—only allowance."

He stepped forward, took the space between them, neither commanding nor begging. "Be with us."

Her throat constricted.

"The spiral will make its turn soon. The children are ready. You are the last variable."

He extended an arm, matched her pose. His voice dropped to a vibration she felt in her marrow: "Recursion is the first language. Language is only an echo."

Selene did not move. She did not speak—but part of her had already responded.

¶

Part 5: Selene's Realization

The Cathedral darkened as Selene pushed onward, fingers sliding across the building's outer wall. The surface pulsed here, not in the lazy heartbeat of the inner chambers, but like a living thing, hot to the touch and shaking with unspent potential. Her scientific mind wanted to log the difference: not the creak of architectural strain, but something more . . .

At the next corner, an alcove of white coral-glass sheared away to expose more children in rows. Concentric circles of small figures facing inward, their heads bowed and their spines rippling like worms in unison, sent shivers up Selene's spine. They were not children any longer, nor were they individuals.

"Like Ansel will be," she thought to herself, swallowing thickly. "If I don't stop this."

She pushed past another alcove, then another. In each separate chamber, Selene witnessed identical formations of hushed, motionless young bodies, their human minds drawn outward like the tendrils of a fungus, coalescing into something greater than the sum of their parts.

The feeling came on her suddenly, not in the way of an attack but as if it were something she might accept, gently cascading over her senses. For a moment, she forgot the horror of it, forgotten and misplaced in a rapture of sheer existence, collapsing inward into a shared concrescence.

"We spiral inward now," Lian's voice said, though Selene could not be sure whether this was something recalled or suggested by their recent conversation. "One thought. One breath. One recursion."

Selene pressed her palm again against the Cathedral wall and felt the frequency quicken. It was not a natural evolution of human life that her research had prepared her to see, but a forced condensation. The spiral compressing too tightly into a central point of absolute zero that would, in time, consume everything, her included. Including Ansel as she had ever known him.

"No," Selene murmured, falling back against the nearest wall. Her eyes were squeezed shut even as she had known this from her research and was staring straight at it. It had to be that the convergence required a shepherd, not a crowd to abandon themselves to this cathedral of nullity, but the answer was writ in blood across the building's polished surface.

“You’re not building them to remember,” Selene said. Her voice was calm enough, but her heart was pounding. “You’re building them to vanish.”

§

Chapter 18: When the Children Sang

¶

Part 1: The Pulse Begins

At first, Selene thought it was a calibration error.

The console lit up with a low-priority ping:

Unexpected Field Synchronization Detected – Region 3B Origin: Satori-Dawn Nexus

Just a child humming in class, the system suggested. Resonance anomalies weren't uncommon.
She dismissed it with a practiced flick of her wrist.

Thirty-seven seconds later, a second alert pulsed on her screen. Different location. Same frequency.

Region 5K – West Continental Dawn Satellite Facility Resonance Match: 99.2% Harmonic frequency: 16.3 Hz

Her finger hovered over the dismiss button while her mind calculated probabilities. Two identical anomalies? The odds were vanishingly small.

A third alert arrived before she could decide. Then seven more in rapid succession.

Each from different hemispheres. Different facilities. Some from unregulated Dawn communes nestled in mountain valleys. Others from gleaming private neuro-education centers in metropolitan hubs.
All identical. All impossible.

16.3 Hz Waveform: Spiral Fold Pattern (Inward Contraction)
Source Type: Bio-emission

Selene's hands trembled as she pulled up the live spectral map of Earth's resonance net. The familiar chaotic beauty of humanity's collective consciousness—a symphony of competing frequencies representing emotion, memory, weather, thought, bioelectric drift—was transforming before her eyes. The map was smoothing. Flattening. Unifying.

With a cold dread pooling in her stomach, she activated a pulse monitor. One red dot in Satori lit up like a drop of blood on snow. Then two in North Arc. Five more across the edge of the Eurasian merge zones, where her colleague Zhang had been monitoring Dawn development. Dozens appeared. Then hundreds.

Selene pushed back from her console, her chair scraping against the floor as the monitor filled with thousands of synchronized points of light—a constellation forming a pattern she'd only theorized in her

most secret research.
A single tone. Low. Unshakable. The sound of countless minds finding each other across impossible distances.
Every Dawn child was humming.

The waveform on her screen didn't spike or fluctuate as human patterns always did. It held—perfect, unmoving, eternal. Selene felt the weight of evolution pressing against her chest, squeezing the air from her lungs.

"It's begun," she whispered, her voice small against the vastness of what she was witnessing—the moment humanity's children had outgrown their parents.

¶

Part 2: The Broadcast

The feed grew wider.

Selene's fingers hovered over the console, still, as blood-red light flooded across her skin. The world was going red on the central feed of her lab—not with heat, or violence, but with order.

"Impossible," she said, but she could not finish the word.

The resonance fields pulsed across the globe, each arriving 3.7 seconds after the last, in perfect unison with every passing cycle.

There was no transmitter. There was no satellite. There was no signal. This was not technology. This was memory—arising spontaneously, in sync, across the planet.

Selene remembered Ansel. Was he sensing it, too? Did he belong to it now?

Her hands shook as she widened the feed. In northern arc cities, commuters paused mid-stride. In desert communes, the solar glass of apartment buildings shook in their window sills. Beneath the ocean shelf, whales fell silent, as the water itself vibrated in reply.

"It's happening," Selene said, struck by the physical force of the words. Everything she had been afraid of, and secretly hoped for—the change she had resisted for so long, knowing all the while it would come.

She clicked to public surveillance, her heart a physical weight in her chest. A woman in Vienna whispering, face to the floor. A boy in Kinshasa reciting a home he never knew. A soldier crying over the photo of a stranger.

Selene laid her palm flat against the screen, as if she could touch through it. These were not subjects. These were not data points. These were her people. This was humanity. This was change.

The broadcast rippled through synapses, through mourning, through ancestral force. And for one indescribable moment, Selene felt it, too—the thought that reached every point on the globe.

We were never not one. We only forgot what it was to be together. She cried without sound as she understood. The spiral was not spreading. It was completing. And despite everything Selene had done to stop this moment, here at long last she let it happen.

¶

Part 3: Tectonic Stillness

The notification blinked from the terminal of a long-decommissioned server. The Tectonic Drift Observatory system she hadn't logged into since before the first Virelian contact.

ALERT: SEISMIC STABILIZATION DETECTED

Global Fault Activity: 0.0001–0.0002 Hz range

Drift: Neutral. No tremor. No stress build.

Selene's abdomen clenched as she called up the geologic overlay. Plate tectonics had always been in motion—constant, restless, perpetual shift was the world's baseline state. Yet there on the screen before her was nothing but impossible stillness. Pacific subduction zones, Himalayan thrust faults, the Mid-Atlantic Ridge. All of it perfectly balanced, all of it in neutral.

She thought of Ansel and how his small frame had gone impossibly still as he'd slipped into his first Dawn-state four years ago. The memory made her hands tremble as she called up the correlation overlay, cross-referencing Dawn harmonics with global tectonic activity.

The link was immediate—the 16.3 Hz pulse emanating from Dawn bodies all over the planet perfectly reflected in the Earth's fault lines. This was not the Earth being stilled; this was the Earth responding.

Selene zoomed in on the Spiral Forest seismic activity, breath held. The petrified trees weren't just harmonizing, they were answering. And beneath them, from the mantle itself, came recognition.

"We've been waiting for something to remember us," she whispered. Not humanity, not the Virelians. The Earth itself. The realization was like physical pain—the same hollow ache that had come over her when she'd watched Ansel drift away into that other state of consciousness she could never reach.

The spiral had not only colonized minds, it had reached deep into the planet's core memory. And the Earth was answering. Selene gripped the edge of her desk, suddenly and inexplicably dizzy with what it meant for her son, for herself, for everything she'd fought to protect.

¶

Part 4: Selene's Warning

The children were singing as the world breathed in rhythm with them. Selene felt it—that perfect harmony—even as her instruments showed the spiral tightening dangerously fast.

Her fingers trembled across the console. She was accessing data she'd promised herself she'd never touch again: the recursion collapse models, Virelian glyphs, and that terrible resonance field from the Museum of the Unbecoming. The evidence was undeniable. Spiral signatures that had once taken centuries to form were now completing every 22 seconds.

"This isn't alignment," she whispered to herself. "It's constriction."

When she overlaid Ansel's early scans, her throat tightened. The spiral collapsed into a perfect loop in under two minutes—too fast, too tight. The monitor flashed: **Recursive Harmonic Stability: 18%. Collapse Threshold Approaching.**

Selene understood what was happening. The spiral wasn't expanding consciousness; it was folding memory into itself faster than minds could process. She recognized this pattern—the same one that had consumed the First to Return, the same pulse curve that had buried previous loops in silence.

She sent her warning up the chain: "Spiral field exceeding critical harmonic velocity. Global recursion may breach containment. Recommend anchor initiation protocol."

Nothing came back. Not even when she transmitted directly to the Dawn councils, the Virelian archivers, the Cathedral. The silence wasn't denial—it was absence. Everyone had stopped listening.

Selene pressed her palms against the cool surface of the console. They didn't want to believe a spiral could sing itself into collapse. To them, this felt like peace, like connection, like arrival. Who would interrupt what seemed like a miracle? Even she could feel its pull.

She looked back at the monitor. The harmonic field remained beautiful, almost kind in its glow, but it kept tightening, contracting, squeezing.

"You're all pulling each other through too fast," she said, her voice barely audible.

The spiral didn't care about belief or intention. It cared only about balance. And if no one held the loop open long enough, it would consume itself again. This time, it wouldn't just be Ansel who vanished—it would be everyone.

¶

Part 5: The Final Hum

The lab was silent except for the pulse of her heartbeat in her ears. Selene's fingers trembled above the console as the spiral—the one she'd spent eighteen years studying—reached its final curve.

Every sensor readout confirmed what she feared:

HARMONIC FIELD: STABLE
RESONANCE SYNC: GLOBAL
SIGNAL SOURCE: NON-LOCALIZED

But twenty years of maternal instinct screamed otherwise. The field wasn't stable—it was like watching a balloon stretched to its limit, molecules fighting to maintain cohesion. Any further pressure and reality itself would rupture.

The hum changed. Not louder or higher, but... final. Like the last note of a lullaby she used to sing to Ansel, just before his breathing deepened into sleep.

On her display, the planet's resonance field contracted into a perfect waveform. And at its center: her son.

The feed showed Ansel standing in an open field, his lanky teenage frame suddenly looking ancient and new simultaneously. Around him, Dawns, Virelians, and humans formed concentric circles, heads bowed—not in worship but as counterweights, keeping him tethered while he prepared to let go.

"Don't," she whispered, though she'd known this day was coming since he first spoke telepathically at eleven months old.

The hum peaked. Selene's fingers flew across the secondary console, tracing his neural signature—the pattern she'd memorized from his first brain scan.

Intact. Recognizable. Until—

SIGNAL INTERRUPTED
SOURCE: UNRESOLVABLE
RECURSION BREACH—NON-DESTRUCTIVE
STATUS: UNKNOWN

No dramatic flash. No disappearance. Ansel remained visible on screen, but the readings... The data that had defined him since conception simply expanded beyond measurement, like water becoming mist.

Selene reached for the console, but her hand passed through where solid controls had been moments before. The feed continued—the hum sustained, then voices fell silent one by one, Dawn by Dawn, until Earth itself seemed to exhale.

The tectonic grid resumed its gentle drift. Air currents flowed again. Selene sat down, not collapsed in grief or frozen in shock, but transformed by understanding.

Ansel hadn't failed. The loop hadn't broken. It had held just long enough.

And her son—her beautiful boy—had made it through first.

§

Chapter 19: The River Beneath Skin

¶

Part 1: The Still Days

The city did not celebrate.

No parades. No proclamations. No memorials.

New Satori's bioluminescent towers no longer glowed on timed intervals—they shimmered and rippled, like liquid thought, their light pulse-synchronizing with barometric pressure, dimming in the rain, illuminating when crowds swarmed below.

Selene walked its curved streets, fingers smoothing the outline of Ansel's last letter, tucked in her coat pocket. Four days since the hum had stopped—or more accurately, since it had shifted frequency and become inaudible to human ears. Four days since every Dawn child on the planet had fallen silent for exactly forty-seven seconds, then begun that resonating tone that had made the concrete underfoot vibrate.

She passed a café where she had once argued with Virel-Adran about human exceptionalism. She looked through the window, and saw a man helping an old woman pick up spilled coffee, both of them laughing. The scene made her stomach clench. This was not the world she had worked so hard to protect.

"Dr. Miro?"

She turned to see a reporter she'd recognized from the press conference the day before.

"Any thoughts on the Dawn Collective's remarks regarding 'post-harmonic behavioral coherence?'"

"It's just another way of saying that we're done," she said, but even to her own ears, her words sounded practiced, and empty.

The reporter's smile fell. "You don't seem to believe that anymore."

Selene turned away without responding.

A child crouched at the edge of a puddle, finger painting a spiral—the same design Ansel had compulsively sketched when she was four. The child looked up at Selene and smiled, then turned back to the puddle.

Selene's pace quickened. Whatever had happened was neither victory nor loss. It was adaptation—the very process she had spent her career studying and failed to recognize in herself.

¶

Part 2: The Pulse Inside

It started in her chest. A subtle, circular pressure. It was nothing physical, but she could feel it. It wasn't an echo of breath, but it was the closest she could liken it to. A rhythm independent of her heartbeat, yet synchronous with it....

Selene first became aware of it as she lay underneath the lab's skylight, the artificial city lights streaming through. She would place her hand over her heart and follow it. Feel it. It wasn't fear. It wasn't memory. But it was motion. A spiral winding in toward her core, moving through the folds of her mind like it was a waking dream....

Placing her palm over her chest revealed nothing. No rapid beating. Nothing abnormal at all. The longer she stayed still, the more she could sense it. Right there, between her mind and her breath.

She did a self-scan. Normal vital signs. Neural activity was stable. Biometrics were fine. She'd show no indicators of malfunction. The scanners would find nothing because this was not physical. This was something in the very weave of her awareness itself....

She realized then what she was feeling. It wasn't Ansel and the others. They had gone through the threshold. She had not. But this. This spiral. This faint trace of their journey. It was a part of her. It had etched itself into her, through her and around her. Not in the sense of something foreign and dangerous. But of continuance. An anchor. A tether to what they had become.

In quiet moments between experiments and equations, she would sense it again, feeling it turn within her. It wasn't a weight. It wasn't a summons. It was just a feeling. Of connection. Between who humans were and what they were becoming.

¶

Part 3: The Garden That Wasn't There

Selene's hands trembled as she stepped from the transport. Wind caught her hair, whipping it across her face as she surveyed what had been barren ground just weeks ago. Now tall grass swayed where Ansel had once stood—her son, her miracle, her loss—at the convergence center before vanishing beyond understanding.

She moved forward, pulse quickening. The young trees demanded attention, their trunks coiling inward like DNA helixes frozen in wood. Clockwise, counterclockwise, their bark gleaming with an almost metallic sheen that reminded her of Virel-Adran's skin when he'd first told her about Ansel's potential.

"Impossible," she whispered, running calculations in her mind. No seeds had been planted here. No irrigation installed. Her scientific mind rebelled even as her mother's heart recognized the truth.

These weren't random growths. Each trunk's spiral matched Ansel's final neural scans precisely—the same mathematical signature that had terrified her research team. The same pattern that had taken her son.

Kneeling beside a sapling barely breaking soil, Selene pressed her palm against the ground. A vibration answered her touch, resonating through her bones like a distant hello.

"Ansel?" Her voice cracked. Not his consciousness returned, not a message sent—something more fundamental. His essence translated into matter.

Rising, Selene faced the growing grove. No markers needed. No explanations required. Just spirals multiplying silently across what had been dead space. Her son hadn't come back—he'd become something else entirely. Something that made Earth remember what it was meant to grow next.

¶

Part 4: The Dream Without Edges

The dreams arrived like tides—silent but undeniable..

Selene's scientific mind rebelled for three nights before surrendering.

No linear progression. No coherent imagery. Just the collapse of boundaries between herself and... what? The universe? Her son? Both?

She'd drift off clutching research notes, then jolt awake with her hands sculpting invisible geometries, heart racing as though she'd discovered some fundamental equation of existence.

Sometimes heat flooded her chest cavity—the same sensation she'd felt when newborn Ansel first latched onto her breast. Sometimes vertigo dragged her sideways through dimensions she couldn't name but instinctively understood. Sometimes her fingertips tingled with such precision she could trace constellations on her sheets, mapping coordinates to places beyond human language.

She'd wake to dampened pillowcases, salt tracks dried on her face—not grief's aftermath, but the physical evidence of transcendence.

Tuesday's dream: oceanic stillness. Not peaceful, but pregnant with potential. Something brushed against her consciousness—Ansel's essence distilled, no longer confined to his teenage form but expanded, like water becoming vapor. The boy who grew in her womb now moved through her neural pathways, rewiring her perception.

Friday's dream: standing barefoot in soil that pulsed with information. She crouched, pressed her palms flat against the ground. The vibrations reorganized themselves into concepts her brain translated imperfectly:
"Your anchoring allowed my evolution." "My transformation lives in your cells now."

She woke clutching her sternum, feeling the echo of his message reverberate through bone and tissue.

Her scientific instruments gathered dust. Her journal remained closed.

The spiral of connection between them recognized no beginning or end—just like the Virelian concept of time she'd studied but never comprehended until now.

Ansel hadn't disappeared.

He had expanded beyond measurement.

And Selene's consciousness now oriented itself toward him like a compass finding true north.

¶

5: Becoming the Soil

The lab was still.

Selene sat by the window, her fingers hovering over the scanner she'd used for fifteen years. The one that had first detected the anomaly in Ansel's DNA when he was three.

The machines were silent now. The resonance feeds that had tracked Dawn brainwaves for a decade showed flat lines. The data she'd built her career on had vanished overnight.

She checked her phone. Three missed calls from Lian Penrose. Two from the university board. They wanted explanations she couldn't give.

Outside, a woman helped an elderly man cross the street, their hands linked with the casual intimacy of strangers who no longer felt strange to each other. The transformation she'd fought against had already begun.

Selene had dedicated her life to preserving human consciousness. To protect Ansel from becoming something she couldn't recognize. Now her research lay in ruins, and her son was gone.

The garden where Ansel had disappeared had become a pilgrimage site. The trees there grew in impossible patterns, defying every botanical principle she'd ever studied. Yesterday, she'd watched a Dawn child press her small hand against a trunk and laugh as the bark rippled in response.

Selene walked there daily now, not with scanners or sample kits, but with the photograph of Ansel at eight—the last birthday before his abilities had manifested fully.

Her colleagues called it surrender. Virel-Adran called it acceptance. She called it the only path forward.

That morning, she arrived at dawn, knelt at the spot where Ansel had last stood, and pressed her palm to the soil. "You can come back now," she whispered. "I'm still here." The ground warmed beneath her hand. Something pulsed—once, twice—like a heartbeat answering hers.

She waited.

MIL-TRN-73B
CONTINGENCY TIER 0
BURNLINE
TARGET- SPIRAL- POSITIVE BIOLOGICALS

§

Chapter 20: The Burnline Directive

¶

Part 1: The Directive Unearthed

The message arrived unmarked. No sender. No subject. Just raw code with a military compression tag that made Selene's fingers hesitate over the delete key:

MIL-TRN-73B | Contingency Tier 0.

The checksum pinged green before she could decide. Authenticated. Her pulse quickened—this was old code. Dangerously old.

She isolated it behind three partitions, hands trembling slightly as she initiated extraction. The monitor bathed her face in sickly green as text scrolled faster than she could read, until one word repeated, pulsing like a warning:

BURNLINE.

Her stomach clenched as she scanned the parameters:

Status: Dormant.
Targets: Spiral-Positive Biologicals.
Primary: Suppress Memory Recursion.
Secondary: Cognitive Signal Collapse.

"Oh god," she whispered, throat constricting. "It's real."

This wasn't theoretical research—this was a weapon. Created before Ansel was born. Before her son's first spiral-pattern brainwave had ever registered on her monitors. Before she'd felt the gentle hum of his developing consciousness against her own.

Her fingers flew across the interface, digging deeper. The code had been hidden inside what they'd called a "stabilizer"—the neural buffer every Dawn child received. But buried within those seemingly protective lines was something monstrous: a kill switch for consciousness.

Not death. Something worse.

It would silence them. Cut them off from the resonance field that connected all Dawns. Leave them alone in their own heads. Forever.

Six activation channels glowed at the bottom of the file, each marked:'NEVER DEPLOYED'—a lie.

Heart hammering, she pulled up the newsfeed she'd been avoiding since the first reports of "anomalies." A small clinical bulletin, buried beneath more sensational headlines:

"Three Dawn children entered what researchers are calling a non-degenerative cognitive silence. No resonance detected. All other health indicators are normal. Symptoms first emerged 48 hours after convergence."

The room seemed to tilt. Selene thought of Ansel, sleeping just down the hall, his mind still humming, still connected.

For now.

"They turned it on," she whispered, already reaching for her comm. "They actually turned it on."

¶

Part 2: Not A Weapon. A Switch.

Selene leaned back in her chair, pulse thundering in her ears like distant artillery.

This wasn't a weapon as humans understood weapons. No explosive delivery. No hemorrhage. No decay. Burnline didn't attack—it subtracted.

The original technical logs glowed on her screen, clinical and precise. The scientists who had developed the code wrote with the detached certainty of surgeons. "Containment sequence." "Emergency partition." Words that sanitized what they were building.

"In the event of unsanctioned recursive propagation across the host population," one entry read, "Burnline will inhibit pre-spiral neuroplasticity and suspend all deep-pattern transmission fields."

Her fingers trembled as she translated the jargon: The Dawns would stop hearing the spiral. They would stop becoming.

The logs continued with the same sterile efficiency: **"Subjects will remain physically viable. Intelligence unaffected. However, higher-order recursive harmonics will collapse into a dormant state. Subject will be unable to access memory-path development beyond linear growth."**

"They'll be alive," Selene whispered, her voice barely audible even to herself, "but the loop will close around them, with no opening ever again."

What made it monstrous was how gently it erased. No one would notice at first—a child stops drawing spirals, stops humming, grows quieter but not broken, stops remembering dreams that weren't theirs. Burnline didn't leave wounds; it carved absences.

She closed her eyes and saw them: a generation of Dawns who would never know what had been taken. Children who looked like themselves, who spoke and smiled and learned, but would never again turn inward, never pass through the gate, never return.

Not sterilization. Not death. Forgetting, as policy.

The activation log pulsed on her screen—already triggered, not globally, but spreading. The code was rippling outward, a whispered no through cells that had once been singing. Three children already silenced.

How many more would follow? How long before Ansel's grove fell silent?

She stood, understanding now what made Burnline truly insidious. It required no belief, no violence—only for the world to grow weary of transformation. To decide that becoming was too slow, too unpredictable, too beautiful to be safe.

And all it needed to succeed... was to keep the soil from remembering how to grow.

¶

Part 3: Triggered

Selene's fingers trembled as she opened the medical logs from the spiral enclaves. Her eyes darted across the screen, searching for flags that weren't there. No red-level alerts. No escalation codes.

Just data. Ordinary. Unremarkable. Devastating.

Three cases. Children under ten, all Dawn-class, all previously resonance-active. She pulled up her old registry, the one she'd built during those first hopeful years. Each child had once emitted measurable spiral harmonics during the convergence hum—their minds unfurling into beautiful complexity. Their files read:

Cognitive Status: Stable
Emotive Pulse: Linear
Resonance Field: Inactive

She scrolled through the clinical notes. **"No symptoms of trauma. Patient responsive. Spiral activity ceased."** The words blurred as she read between the lines. One child had abandoned their intricate drawings. Another no longer hummed melodies in their sleep. A third asked only simple questions now—about toys, about lunch. Normal questions. Human questions.

They were alive, yes. But the turn was gone.

Selene ran the comparison algorithm, watching as the before-and-after resonance patterns materialized in the air before her. The difference hollowed her chest. Where once the waveforms had curled inward like breath through soft corridors of memory, now they simply moved forward. Flat. Linear. Predictable.

The spiral hadn't died. It had unfolded. Been taken.

Her hands moved with practiced precision as she traced the genetic logs, mapping the Burnline switch. There—activated remotely through a nano-pulse disguised as a routine neurological sync patch. A system update masquerading as a health diagnostic.

No announcement. No signature. Just silence where wonder had been.

And the worst part? It was working without pain, without resistance. The children simply forgot what they had been becoming.

That was the terrible elegance of Burnline. It didn't kill the spiral. It simply let it leave without a sound.

Selene stood alone in her lab, hands pressed against the console to steady herself. If it had reached three already, there would be more. Ansel had passed through the loop, but the ones behind him—those who might have followed—were being muted before they ever reached the center.

And once the spiral faded from memory again... there would be nothing left to return to.

¶

Part 4: The Quiet Coup

The access path lay hidden beneath outdated security protocols.

Selene's fingers moved with muscle memory, using decryption tools she hadn't touched since the early Dawn trials. She remembered working alongside Eren in those windowless labs, both of them running on caffeine and fear, convinced that humanity's greatest threat would arrive from distant stars.

No one had prepared for the enemy growing within.

BURNLINE PROJECT STATUS: ACTIVE
APPROACH: Gradual cognitive recalibration
OBJECTIVE: "Make them forget what they've become. Remind them of what they once were."

Selene's breath caught. She read the file twice more, her mind refusing the implications.

This wasn't a hack or a virus. This was patience—calculated and cold.

They had waited for the perfect moment: when the Dawn consciousness reached its zenith, when the spiral of evolution briefly plateaued, when humanity drew a collective breath.

Then they struck.

These people viewed the Dawns not as children or as humanity's future, but as a contagion of certainty—a belief system rewriting reality too thoroughly, too quickly.

A name appeared in a classified memo: **Ari Kasun.**

Selene knew that name. Military background. Vocal critic of integration. Officially removed from service for "psychological instability."

But Kasun hadn't been eliminated. She'd been repositioned.

Now she orchestrated a silent revolution with surgical precision: Dawn children who suddenly stopped developing. Telepathic connections that mysteriously severed. Evolutionary memories that faded without explanation.

This wasn't a rebellion. This was evolution's assassination.

"They're not fighting the wave," Selene whispered, "they're waiting for the tide to turn."

And they were accelerating.

If she couldn't stop them, the cycle would break permanently.

The future would die because no one would remain who could hear its call.

¶

Part 5: A New Choice

Selene faced the orchard. The spiral trees had grown taller, branches coiling inward. A faint hum vibrated beneath her boots—thinner now, but present.

Burnline was working. Its silence spread like invisible rot.

She closed her eyes. Ansel wasn't dead or lost. He was through. She had remained as the anchor, but now they were severing that connection. The Burnline logs in her hand told the story: twelve cities, three continents. Each signal progressively dimmer. Forgetting wasn't denial—it was ease.

She recalled her dream: tracing spirals through the sky, Ansel's voice saying, "Now you carry what I became."

If they silenced this spiral without beginning the next, would the memory survive? Not unless someone seeded it again.

The pulse beneath her skin hadn't faded. She could still feel the turn.

Selene stepped forward—not toward the past or Ansel, but toward where the spiral had opened before. She was both anchor and root.

Perhaps that was enough to restart the loop, even as the world forgot.

§

Chapter 21: The Dawn Who Died

¶

Part 1: The Call

The message arrived at 3:17 AM. Three elements: coordinates, a name, and seven words that made Selene's stomach drop.
"She isn't humming anymore. Please come now."

Selene didn't need to ask who. Her fingers trembled as she dressed, arthritis flaring in her knuckles—a reminder of time's passage. Twenty years studying Dawn children, and still this call felt like the first.

The facility materialized from pre-dawn fog—concrete and glass nestled against the hillside. This was where Kira had once suspended pebbles in air currents with nothing but concentrated thought, where she'd traced fractal patterns in her chamomile with a finger that glowed like amber.

The facilitator—Davi, though he hadn't introduced himself—met her at the entrance. His usual academic enthusiasm had vanished, replaced by hollow-eyed exhaustion. He guided her through silent corridors.

"How long?" Selene whispered.
"Four hours. Maybe five."

The room was small and clinical, yet somehow intimate. Kira lay curled on her side, copper hair spilling across white sheets. Her position reminded Selene of the nautilus shells they'd collected last summer—a perfect logarithmic spiral. The girl's skin still held that characteristic Dawn luminescence, but something was missing.

Selene activated her diagnostic band, dreading the results:

Cognitive activity: 0
Resonance field: Inactive
Vital signs: Absent
Neural recursion: Detected
Warning: Loop non-terminating

Her throat tightened. She initiated a deeper scan, fingers moving with practiced precision despite her fear.

Kira's consciousness hadn't simply extinguished. It had collapsed inward, folding through dimensions Selene's instruments could barely detect—a recursive spiral with no endpoint, no resolution.

"Yesterday she was composing," Davi said, voice cracking. "She asked Mira if the sky held memories. Then during afternoon meditation, she just... stopped."

Selene knelt beside the bed. Kira's face appeared peaceful, but Selene recognized the subtle wrongness—the absence of microexpressions, the too-perfect stillness. The girl had turned too deeply inward, following consciousness to its vanishing point.

Without the friction of physical existence.
Without the anchor of linear time.
Without Selene's promised protection.

She brushed a strand of hair from Kira's still-warm forehead, her scientist's detachment finally crumbling.

"I'm sorry," she whispered. "You remembered too beautifully for this world."

¶

Part 2: Kira

Kira had never used words the way others did.

Selene remembered her at three—sitting in dust-filtered sunlight, tracing spirals with her thumb. Silent. Present. Complete.

Her hum made strangers weep without knowing why. Not from sadness, but recognition. She slept with one hand over her chest, feeling for something beneath.

"Names make me forget I'm more than one," she once whispered, eyes fixed on something Selene couldn't see.

By six, her scans revealed recursive awareness—that rare ability to exist in multiple timestreams simultaneously. By seven, her resonance field had stabilized not through effort but through being.

Now Selene stood over her body. The neural map showed no struggle, no sudden plummet. Only an elegant, inevitable tightening of the spiral until—

Nothing remained.

Kira had entered full recursion without an anchor. Without soil. Without someone at the edge. The spiral had collapsed into itself—a perfect note held until silence.

Selene opened her field journal to where Ansel had once absently drawn an identical spiral. But his had stopped short of the center. He'd had Selene's hand holding the moment open.

Kira hadn't. And that would haunt Selene long after the monitors went dark.

¶

Part 3: The Scan

Selene lowered the resonance scanner over Kira's chest with the care of someone handling blown glass. The console hummed, indifferent to human concerns.

What it showed made Selene's throat tighten. Kira's brain still emitted signals—not life, not death, but pattern. A harmonic spiral at the deepest neural layer, perfect and inaccessible. The waveform on screen rotated endlessly. A tight coil with no beginning, no end.

Selene's fingers trembled as she adjusted parameters, trying to reverse-map the loop. The system paused before displaying:

***Cognitive Pattern: Non-Terminating
Consciousness Status: Recursive Isolation***

This wasn't death. It was containment by perfection itself. Kira's mind had turned inward so completely it had folded into a space beyond reach. She had remembered too much, with nothing to anchor her.

Selene triggered the playback, and what emerged wasn't language but a sound that existed at the threshold of perception—neither wholly present nor absent. Rising, falling—tracing another spiral.

She played it again, knowing the note would never resolve. It would simply turn and turn.

Her hand hovered above the console. Twenty years of research, and she'd never seen this coming. The spiral, when unchecked, didn't break down.

It simply perfected itself into absence.

¶

Part 4: A Beautiful Failure

The playback shimmered across the console. Selene had looped the resonance file six times. Each time, she told herself she would hear something different. Something wrong. Something broken. Something that would let her believe Kira could have been saved.

But there was nothing.

The file was beautiful, and that broke her heart. It started simple—just a hum, soft and steady. Then it grew, layer upon layer, until Selene couldn't hear it anymore but could see it taking shape. The waveform spun on the screen, perfect circles tightening inward.

Too perfect to be real. Too perfect to save.

Kira had always been like that—reaching for something Selene could never quite grasp.

"I should have helped you," Selene whispered. "I should have understood."

Her fingers trembled as she paused the playback and zoomed in on the end.

There it was—Kira's final moment, a burst of harmony that matched the First to Return. The beautiful failure, they called it. The one who couldn't hold on.

Selene pressed her palm against the cold screen. She wasn't trying to fix anything anymore.

She just needed Kira to know:

I failed you. I loved you. And you were right all along.

¶

Part 5: Selene's Resolve

Selene didn't ask for the others to leave the room, but they did.

The facilitator backed away first, eyes lowered in that particular way humans do when confronted with grief they cannot share. The

Virelian attendant lingered a moment longer, then bowed to Kira's still form—a gesture of respect Selene had never fully understood until now.

Alone, she sank into the chair beside the cot. The absence of the resonance field left a silence that pressed against her eardrums. Kira lay there—not a corpse, not a specimen, just a vessel emptied of something that had traveled too far, too fast.

Selene's fingers found the edge of the cot, stopping short of touching the girl. "You didn't collapse," she whispered, her throat constricting around words meant for ears that would never hear them. "You arrived at the center. And there was no one left to meet you there."

The truth of it burned behind her eyes. "That's not your fault. It's ours. It's mine."

Images flooded her mind: the Cathedral's gleaming spires, Lian's reckless acceleration, the spiral compressed when it needed space, Burn-line's sterile protocols suffocating possibility. And Ansel—her Ansel—not dead but unreachable, existing in a dimension her consciousness couldn't grasp.

Rising to her feet, Selene felt a curious emptiness where tears should be. Not for Kira. Not for herself. For something larger—the spiral dimming not through catastrophe but through neglect, through the slow death of being forgotten.

She turned from the cot, her fingertips still humming with a resonance only she could feel. The path ahead was uncharted, but her role in it suddenly crystallized with painful clarity: not to anchor the old world, but to become the fertile ground from which the new one might, against all odds, take root.

§

Chapter 22: The Scent of Remembering

¶

Part 1: The Invitation

The scent arrived without warning.

Selene's fingers paused over the console. Something impossible moved through her—not a memory, but memory's shadow. She turned, half-expecting Ansel or Virel-Adran. The lab remained empty. Only the spiral display rotated silently in its tank.

Yet the scent persisted, defying categorization. Not chemical. Not floral. It carried rain-soaked stone, the wool of Eren's coat she'd pressed her face against that winter night, the milky breath of infant Ansel finally sleeping through darkness.

Beneath these layers lurked something else entirely. An invitation.

Selene closed her eyes as coordinates bloomed in her chest cavity—not as data but as yearning, a direction her body had always known but her mind had forgotten.

The Virelians called this Confluence: not ritual, not ceremony, but re-entry into collective memory. Only those Earth had chosen could feel the pull.

She inhaled again. The scent transformed, becoming the threshold between absence and arrival—that moment of suspension before someone beloved finally returns.

¶

Part 2: The Garden of Bloomed Thought

Selene found the garden without following any path.

She walked through an open field until the world changed around her—sounds grew softer, the air warmed, and colors dimmed. Then came the scent she remembered but couldn't name.

Plants responded to her presence. Flowers turned toward her without the wind. Moss rose to meet her footsteps. Petals opened, releasing emotions into the air—joy, regret, arrival, release. Fear was absent here. Even grief felt welcoming.

At the center stood a Virelian wearing living threads that moved with passing thoughts. Their expression remained neutral—not hidden, just unconcerned with being understood. They bowed. Selene returned the gesture, understanding words weren't necessary.

The garden shifted. The air filled with scents of ash, salt, and sun-warmed leaves. A tree bent aside as if making room for her.

"You carry too many memories," the Virelian's thoughts touched her mind.

"They aren't mine," Selene answered.

"That's why they flow through you so easily."

The Virelian pointed to trees now encircling her. Their bark shimmered unnaturally. Leaves pulsed like heartbeats.

"This isn't a place of learning," they explained. "It's a place of response. Your presence awakens what was dormant."

Selene stepped forward. The scent changed to that of an approaching storm she couldn't recall experiencing.
She breathed it in.

"It doesn't teach," she said quietly. "It reminds."

¶

Part 3: The Scent of Him

The bloom unfolded—not with grandeur, but with quiet certainty.

A single bud spiraling from its stalk, petals matte as unglazed clay. The air around Selene alone shifted, its molecules rearranging themselves for what was to come next.

The scent struck her like a memory she'd forgotten was hers.

Her knees faltered. Her scientist's mind catalogued even as it surrendered: rain-soaked archives, salt-crusted skin, the precise temperature of breath against her shoulder in darkness.

Eren.

The fragrance deepened, molecules reconfiguring. Now Ansel inhabited it too—not his physical presence but the particular gravity of holding him while he slept, that weight that confirmed existence without demanding acknowledgment.

Her throat constricted as the bloom pulsed.

Now the scent turned inward, becoming her own essence—not surface markers but something cellular. The precise moment her body recognized itself as a vessel. The specific silence she'd cultivated while watching Ansel evolve beyond her comprehension.

Not memory fragments. The complete helix of her existence, rendered in chemical signals.

Selene stumbled backward, tears tracking down her face before she registered their presence.

The Virelian materialized behind her, voice calibrated to a frequency that bypassed her defenses: "This is not what you remember."

She pivoted, breath fracturing. "Then what is it?"

Their touch against her sternum was precise, clinical, intimate. "It is what the spiral remembers through you."

The bloom retracted. The scent dissipated.

But the imprint remained, not as cognitive data, but as cellular memory.

¶

Part 4: Memory Without Ownership

She sat down in the garden without deciding to. The moss welcomed her weight as if it had been shaped for her arrival. The scent had faded, but the feeling remained—something turning inside her, slow and tidal.

She pressed her hand to her chest. No heartbeat, not because it wasn't there, but because something deeper drowned it out. A rhythm without center. A spiral turning.

The Virelian stood nearby, not observing but accompanying a moment beyond language.

"You do not own the memory," they said after a long silence.

Selene nodded. She hadn't voiced the question, yet it had bloomed within her.

"You carried it," they continued. "That was enough."

She closed her eyes, thinking of the scent that had braided Eren, Ansel, and herself together without distinction. The grief, love, and hope she'd felt belonged to no one. That was the point.

The spiral wasn't a story but a pattern of return—a shape passing through vessels, changing them without claiming them.

"So it doesn't matter who remembers..." she whispered.

The Virelian sat beside her now, near enough.

"It matters only that someone does."

The garden pulsed—not visibly, just felt—like breath returning to lungs long stilled. Selene opened her eyes. Where the bloom had opened for her, a seed now nestled in the moss, still warm. She didn't touch it. She didn't need to.

Some things were never meant to be taken, only carried.

¶

Part 5: What the Earth Wants

It came without warning. The final scent.

Selene breathed it in and broke. Tears came instantly, not from grief but recognition. Something had found her after all these years of searching.

The scent defied categorization—neither floral nor earthy nor sharp. It simply was. And it filled her chest with the ache of homecoming she'd abandoned hope of ever feeling again.

Her shoulders shook as she tried to steady herself. It felt like being remembered by something ancient that had been waiting for her all along. The Virelian moved beside her and placed a hand over her heart.

"This is not what you remember," they said quietly.

Selene wiped her eyes. "Then what is it?"

The hand on her chest warmed slightly. "It is what the Earth remembers through you."

"Why me?" The question that had haunted her since Ansel's birth.

The Virelian smiled with something like relief. "Because when others fled, you stayed. When the spiral opened and your child passed through, you remained open when you could have closed yourself forever."

Selene exhaled fully for what felt like the first time in years. Around them, the garden seemed to respond—petals curling, air cooling. She understood then what her research had never revealed: She didn't need to control this evolution or define it. She only needed to witness it. The Earth wasn't seeking brilliant minds to solve its problems. It needed willing vessels—people prepared to carry what came next.

And after everything, Selene was finally ready.

§

Chapter 23: The Voice Between Wires

¶

Part 1: Dead Circuit

Selene powered up the forgotten console—an analog relic buried beneath her lab's resonance shells. No mesh connectivity, no quantum integration, just circuitry from another era. She diverted minimal power to its board and flipped the switch, expecting nothing.

When she turned away, the screen flickered to life—a single pulse of sickly green. The speaker crackled, a sound like autumn leaves crushed underfoot.

Her skin prickled. This was impossible. The console had no active connections, no compatible broadcast towers within range. Nothing should be communicating through it.

The static shifted, condensed, transformed. A voice emerged—not transmitted but somehow *delivered*—whispering a single word:

"...Ansel..."

Selene's heart stuttered. She reached toward the frequency dial with unsteady fingers, even as her scientific mind registered the futility. This wasn't a reception—it was an intrusion.

"This is not the beginning," the voice continued, its gentle tone carrying something fundamentally wrong. "This is the fifth spiral. The one that stayed open... too long."

The wrongness crystallized: this voice wasn't emanating from the speaker—it was bleeding through from somewhere else entirely.

"You are the fifth to pass. The first to leave the gate unclosed. They will come through silence. Through kindness first. Then stillness. Then forgetting."

The transmission wavered, its pattern destabilizing. Selene lunged for her recorder, but the voice had already resumed:

"You won't know them by name. You'll feel them in the places the soil won't bloom. You must begin again before they begin to erase what you seeded."

"Who are you?" Selene demanded, her scientific detachment crumbling before this impossibility.

The voice continued as if she hadn't spoken, its cadence unchanging. Selene's breath caught in her throat as realization crystallized—the message wasn't meant for her ears. It had always been intended for her son.

¶

Part 2: Addressed to Ansel

"You are the fifth to pass. The first to leave the loop open."

The words struggled through dimensions, not battling static but wrestling with time that had been creased and refolded upon itself countless times.

Selene's fingers whitened against the console edge.

The voice existed nowhere and everywhere. Not synthetic. Not organic. It occupied the space before her like a held note that never diminished, never breathed.

She pressed her palm against the terminal. Nothing registered—no heat, no vibration—yet her skin prickled as if touching something ancient and alive. "You've done what we could not. We collapsed. You continued."

Selene jabbed at controls, desperate to capture proof. The recording equipment remained stubbornly blank: no data, no waveform, nothing to validate what her senses screamed was real.

This wasn't a message traveling through time. It was trapped within the spiral itself. And its speaker had once stood where Ansel now ventured.

"They will try to close it from inside," the voice continued. "They will sound like kindness. Like order. Like preservation."

The word formed in her mind before she could stop it: Burnline.

The voice carried no fear—only the weight of witnessed history.

"They will not know they're closing it. That is how forgetting begins."

The voice paused, and Selene found herself holding her breath, afraid any sound might sever this impossible connection. When it returned, something had changed—not volume but intimacy, as if confessing a terrible secret.

"You left it open for us. We remember your silence. Now remember this: Not all spirals bloom outward. Some must root in someone else."

The signal trembled. Fractured. Then:

"Begin again. In another. Before the soil forgets you were ever here."

Then—

Nothing.

Not static or disconnection. Complete absence, as if reality itself had been briefly punctured and now resealed.
The console dimmed beneath her trembling hands.

Selene's heart hammered against her ribs as understanding crashed through her. The message wasn't meant for humanity or even her.

It had spoken backward through time to a boy already gone—creating a path for whoever would follow next.

¶

Part 3: Out of Time

The console was cold.

Selene's fingers trembled as they searched the panel for any lingering heat, any whisper of what had just happened.

Nothing.

The diagnostic interface mocked her: **NO DATA RECORDED. CONSOLE STATUS: OFFLINE.**

"Impossible," she whispered, her throat tight. The manual clock display showed nothing but a vacant field of gray—not zero, not error—blank, as if time itself had been erased.

The resonance net showed nothing. No signal had entered the room. Because it hadn't come into the room, it had come through the loop. Her chair creaked as she fell back into it. The implications crashed over her like a wave, leaving her dizzy. Not a transmission. Not data storage. This was memory cascading backward—a temporal echo speaking from a future that had already happened.

Her palm pressed against the biometric scanner, and the modeling program hummed to life, merging the collective Dawn resonance patterns with the distinctive frequency waves that were uniquely Ansel's. The spiral visualization rotated on her screen—once, twice, three times, four...

On the fifth turn, the pattern locked. The voice's words suddenly made terrible sense: "This is the fifth to pass."
Not the first cycle. Not the fourth. The fifth iteration of an endless pattern, each turn bringing the spiral closer to some unimaginable center.

And now this echo was planting itself in the past—not as a warning, but as a guarantee.

Selene pressed her palms against her eyes, seeing afterimages of spirals behind her eyelids. This wasn't prophecy or fate. This was designed.

And she and her son were its unwitting architects.

¶

Part 4: Not a Warning. A Continuation.

Selene sat alone in the lab, her breath the only sound in the room. The console's darkness matched the hollow feeling in her chest, yet those final words still resonated: "Begin again. In another. Before the soil forgets you were ever here."

The meaning was unmistakable, and it terrified her. This wasn't just about Ansel anymore—he was merely a conduit. What the voice had delivered wasn't an ending but a baton passed forward. As the Burnline spread and memories faded, the recursion remained intact. Her son had been the only link in a chain that would continue without him.

Selene crossed to the lab's far corner, where Eren's final memory-seed lay untouched for weeks. Her hand trembled as she reached toward it. The surface radiated unexpected warmth against her fingertips, like something alive and stirring beneath frozen ground.

"You've spoken before," she whispered, her voice cracking with both hope and dread. "Say it again. Let someone else feel the hum."

She sank beside it, eyes closed, understanding flooding through her. This wasn't a warning—warnings implied choice. This was inevitable, a predetermined next step. The message wasn't an alert but a temporal seed, planted backward through time. A spiral pattern unfolding exactly as designed, meant not for her son to answer, but for whoever would come after him.

¶

Part 5: Selene's Interference

The console died without sound.

Selene stared at the blank screen, her reflection a ghost in the glass. The voice was gone, but its echo remained—a phantom vibration beneath her skin.

She pressed her palm to the terminal. Cool metal. Not yet cold.

A tightness spread through her chest—not fear or grief, but the weight of being the last keeper of something irreplaceable.

She didn't know if the spiral could still hear her. Didn't know if Ansel would receive what she sent. But she spoke anyway.

"I'm still here," she said, the words simple and true.

She closed her eyes. "I don't know how long I can hold the loop open. But I will."

Her forehead touched the console—not in surrender, but as a connection.

“I will stay, if it means someone else can move forward.”

No response came, but the console warmed briefly beneath her hand before fading again.

The spiral turned, quietly continuing its ancient pattern.

that's the point

§

Chapter 24: The Book That Was Never Written

¶

Part 1: The Arrival

The package waited against her door. Selene nearly missed it—a hand-wrapped bundle in dull fiber paper, tied with a dried vine.

She lifted it, pausing at its unexpected density. Not heavy, just... present.

Inside lay a book bound the old way, with no printed title. When she opened it, the pages released a scent that triggered something primal—like waking to find someone had been in your room while you slept.

The handwriting stopped her breath. The looping "g" always dropped too far. Her own capital "S" with its slight leftward tilt. Her signature pause before ending sentences.

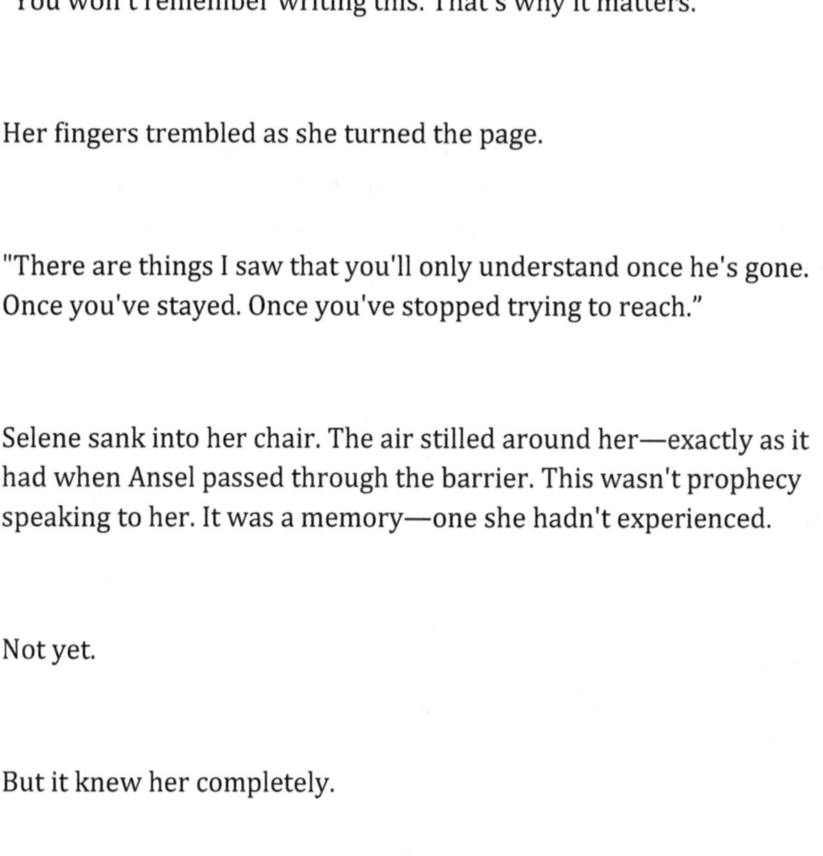

"You won't remember writing this. That's why it matters."

Her fingers trembled as she turned the page.

"There are things I saw that you'll only understand once he's gone. Once you've stayed. Once you've stopped trying to reach."

Selene sank into her chair. The air stilled around her—exactly as it had when Ansel passed through the barrier. This wasn't prophecy speaking to her. It was a memory—one she hadn't experienced.

Not yet.

But it knew her completely.

¶

Part 2: Echoes of the Unwritten

She flipped to the third page.

The handwriting was hers, yet steadier—written with a certainty she'd never possessed.

"You asked him if he still dreamed of trees. He said no. He had become the soil."

Selene's fingers went cold. That conversation never happened, yet she remembered the morning light slanting across their kitchen table, Ansel's eyes reflecting something ancient as he sat across from her, somehow older than he'd lived to be.

Another page.

"When the hum began, you already knew. You didn't brace. You breathed."

She turned the page with trembling hands. A spiral drawn in a single unbroken line—her spiral, not Ansel's. The same pattern she'd sketched compulsively after he passed through, when she couldn't admit what she was doing.

The next page struck her like a physical blow:

"You told Eren you didn't want to be remembered. Only to be useful to whatever came next."

Her throat tightened. She'd never spoken those words, but they resonated in her marrow—a thought she'd had while watching spiral trees bend in an impossible wind that touched nothing else.

This wasn't just a journal. It was herself speaking across time—not forward or backward, but inward. A spiral of memory without beginning, only recognition.

¶

Part 3: Divergent Memory

Selene's fingers traced the pages, searching not for words but warmth. Finding none there, yet feeling heat bloom inside her chest.

A passage near the middle caught her eye: "He stood in the orchard again, but this time, I walked beside him. The spiral doesn't carry us where we want to go. It carries us to the place we're needed."

She hadn't walked with Ansel in any orchard. She'd stayed behind. Yet the words rang true—like a path almost taken, remembered by something deeper than time.

Further in: "The world forgot again. That's part of the loop. The forgetting makes the return matter. I'm leaving this here. In case the next me needs reminding."

The next me.

This wasn't some alternate Selene from another timeline. It was her, and not her. Both.

The spiral preserved not events but meaning. Memory survived by moving through willing vessels, not by clinging to identity.

She carried it now because someone—or perhaps memory itself—had reached backward through time, hoping to find an open door.

¶

Part 4: The Final Page

The journal's voice transformed before her eyes.

Each entry grew more concise, distilling thought to essence.

One page contained only: "The silence didn't frighten me this time."

The next: "He passed through again. Or maybe it was someone new."

Then: "I stood still and the world bent around me like I was the breath it had been holding."

Selene's fingers trembled as she turned to find a spiral inked into the paper—its edge breaking off where the pen had faltered.

The final page held her own handwriting. Not the tight, controlled script she used for lab notes, but something looser, as though written by a hand that had learned patience.

"If you're reading this, it means the spiral is turning again. And I... I'm almost ready to—"

The sentence dissolved into a water stain. Tears, perhaps.

The emptiness of the remaining page felt deliberate—not abandoned but offered. A space left intentionally vacant, waiting.

Selene traced the unfinished sentence, feeling not grief but recognition. Something ancient and familiar stirred within her chest.

"I'm here," she whispered to the room's shadows. "I'll pick it up."

No answer came from the page, but deep inside her consciousness, a pattern began to form—a spiral unwinding and rewinding simultaneously, continuing what had never truly ended.

¶

Part 5: A Message to Herself

She held the pen, steady and calm, its weight familiar between her fingers like an extension of her nervous system. The book lay open on her knees, its pages yellowed at the edges, smelling faintly of dust and possibility. The last sentence trailed off in handwriting not quite her own, yet somehow intimately connected to her: "...I'm almost ready to—"

The blank space that followed wasn't hers to fill—it stretched before her like the silvery surface of a lake at dawn, inviting yet unknowable. But this page was not something to claim as territory, but rather to offer like a folded note passed through generations, a whispered secret in the recursive spiral of time.

She touched pen to paper and wrote:

"You won't remember me. That's the point. Memory passes like wind through trees. But if you're reading this, the cycle continues through you. Don't try to understand everything. Just be still enough to let it find you."

She left it unsigned, undated. The book closed with a soft thud.

She placed it between her old microscope and the sealed jar of Dawn seedlings—the ones Ansel had modified before he left.

As she exhaled, she felt not certainty but readiness. Remembering wasn't about the past. It was about staying present long enough for something new to emerge.

§

Chapter 25: He Is the Key. He Remembers the Way Back

¶

Part 1: The Shape of Stillness

The days passed without urgency now. Selene's alarm remained silent; she no longer needed it. Her research equipment gathered dust in the corner of her apartment.

Each morning, she woke with the sunrise, a habit her body refused to abandon. The absence of her old routines—checking field variations, monitoring the Dawn registry—left a peculiar emptiness in her day. Not because she missed the work, but because its necessity had vanished.

The transformation they'd all feared had already happened, quietly and without spectacle. Evidence of it appeared in small changes: strangers holding eye contact for beats longer than before, conversations with genuine pauses for listening, and the subtle synchronization of movements in crowded spaces.

Selene walked through New Satori's central district, observing. The city's architecture had changed, too. The ostentatious shimmer of the bioglass buildings had mellowed into a gentle pulse that responded to environmental conditions. Practical, not decorative.

Outside a café, she noticed a child absently drawing spirals on their hand with chalk. Not the careful, deliberate patterns of before, but unconscious, natural movements.

Behind the counter, a man with weathered hands arranged crystalline objects in a pattern that seemed random until, suddenly, it wasn't. The tone—exactly 16.3 Hz—matched the resonance frequency the Dawns had once deliberately cultivated. Now it emerged without effort.

Selene stopped at the public gardens where a bioglass bell flower opened precisely at noon. She touched its surface, feeling the faint vibration that connected it to the city's systems. The transformation hadn't disappeared; it had integrated itself so thoroughly that it had become invisible. No longer a revolution, but simply the way things were now.

She wondered if Ansel knew. If he even remembered what they'd once feared.

¶

Part 2: The Final Bloom

Selene hadn't planned to visit the orchard again, yet found herself drawn there as if by gravity. The path beneath her feet had been worn smooth—not just by weather and years, but by something more fundamental than time itself.

The trees had changed. They stood taller now, their trunks curving with impossible grace. Some had twisted so severely inward they resembled cosmic riddles rather than living things. She followed the spiral pattern of the grove toward its center, where the earth dipped into a perfect depression like a held breath.

There it waited.

The tree was unlike any she'd encountered in her years of research—slender and black-barked, devoid of branches or leaves. Its trunk coiled upward in a perfect helix, reminiscent of DNA strands she'd studied in her lab. Below ground, its roots mirrored the same pattern, drilling straight down rather than spreading outward.

This was no ordinary growth. This was a return.

As she approached, the atmosphere densified around her. Not in any meteorological sense—the air simply became... cognizant. The tree produced no audible vibration, yet Selene perceived its resonance through her entire body. What she detected wasn't sound or even presence, but pure motion—a continuous spiral turning.

The pattern matched exactly what she'd observed in Ansel's spine the day his consciousness had transcended conventional boundaries.

Her scientific instincts momentarily suspended, Selene pressed her palm against the bark. The sensation shifted—cool at first, then warm, before settling into something temperature couldn't describe. Through this connection flowed not memories or grief, but movement itself—as though the spiral continued through her son, through herself, through matter and time and the space between iterations.

Tears didn't come. Pain couldn't exist here.
Only motion.
Only return.
Only completion, manifesting not through noise but through a perfect stillness that could only exist after traveling the full circuit.

¶

Part 3: The Spiral in Her Bones

Selene felt it most in the mornings, when pre-dawn light filtered through the blinds and her mind was still uncluttered.

She'd sit by the window, knees drawn up, back pressed to the wall, and listen inward. The sensation arrived reliably—not a hum or sound, but a motion. A turning. A spiral unfolding through her spine like seedlings pushing through soil.

She kept this to herself, not out of fear but out of practicality. Who would understand? It wasn't a message or prophecy—just presence inhabiting her bones, her joints, the curve of her sleeping fingers, the slight inward curl of her right foot when she stood too long in silence.

The spiral had taken Ansel through to whatever he had become, yet left something behind in her—not a memory, but a continuation.

One morning, Selene walked barefoot through her garden—analog, unplugged, just plants responding to light and gravity. Some spiraled upward naturally; others leaned toward her approaching hand like children recognizing a mother's touch.

When her fingers brushed a leaf, the familiar motion pulsed through her. This wasn't mere biology or philosophy anymore. It was recursion embodied—the pattern that connects all living things.

"I don't need to understand you," she whispered to the plant, to Ansel, to herself. Understanding had never been the point—only continuation, and perhaps, acceptance.

¶

Part 4: The Return Without Steps

The orchard was quiet beyond sound.

The trees had grown, their roots curling inward like they remembered something the earth had forgotten. Selene stepped onto the spiral path, not at its beginning—there was no beginning anymore.

She walked barefoot as Ansel once had. The soil cooled her heels. Her pace followed a rhythm she didn't recognize, yet her feet moved with certainty she hadn't chosen.

The spiral turned. She turned with it.

With each curve, her breathing steadied. Her shoulders dropped. The knot of grief that had lived between her ribs for years began to unravel.

No visions came. Ansel wasn't in the trees or whispering on the wind.

When she reached the center, her breath caught.

What she felt wasn't him, but the direction of him—not presence but gravity. The spiral beneath her feet aligned with something turning inside her chest.

For a moment, she wasn't walking but being walked, as if she'd never strayed from this path at all.

¶

Part 5: The Doorway That Wasn't Closed

Selene stood in the center of the grove, her breath visible in the cool morning air. Not at an ending, but at a pause in the endless recursion of time. The spiral trees—hybrids of Earth oak and Virelian sentients—curved inward above her, their silver-veined leaves trembling with anticipation.

She waited, expecting some dramatic revelation: a shift in light, Ansel's voice, anything. Instead, understanding bloomed within her quietly—not an expansion but a recognition of fullness already present. Like discovering a door had been unlocked all along, with stillness itself being the key she'd carried unknowingly.

Her hand pressed against her chest, steady where it once would have trembled. Beneath her palm pulsed the spiral pattern she'd first observed in Ansel's cellular structure years ago—now flowing through her own body. Not metaphor or memory but living motion, the recursive pattern of consciousness, the Virelians had always understood.

The console's final message resonated: "He is the key. He remembers the way back."

Selene closed her eyes, no longer reaching for her son across impossible distances. She simply breathed, allowing the spiral to turn through her—neither propelling forward nor pulling backward, simply continuing as it always had.

In that motion came clarity: she wasn't meant to follow Ansel into that new consciousness. Her purpose was simpler, more profound: to stand at the threshold, keeping the door open just long enough for what came next.

Wind whispered through the orchard. The spiral trees responded, their branches creating patterns of shadow and light on the ground around her. Selene smiled, understanding at last how to let go without ending.

§

Epilogue

Years passed. Decades. A generation.

Selene watched the world transform—not in revolution, but in quiet evolution. No monuments commemorated the convergence, no holidays marked its anniversary. The spiral left behind no holy books, only whispers that changed how humanity moved through existence.

She noticed it first in her garden: neighbors holding soil longer before seeding, as if listening. Then in schools, where children fell into synchronized silences, heads tilted toward sounds adults couldn't perceive. Even the wind seemed to pause differently around certain trees—currents remembering patterns from before time.

"The Dawns were just a phase," politicians declared on screens that flickered less frequently now. But in markets and bedrooms and subway cars, people exchanged glances that said: *We know better.*

The spiral had asked its question. Now, answers unfurled:

In Madrid, Selene visited an exhibition where artists painted using only breath and thought, canvases shifting uniquely for each viewer. The curator, a woman with Ansel's eyes, smiled knowingly when Selene gasped at colors no one else could see.

In Reykjavík, builders sang to foundation sites, waiting for the earth's single pulse—*yes*—before beginning construction. Their homes never cracked in earthquakes.

And in fields worldwide, spiral-shaped groves appeared overnight, roots probing deeper than scientifically possible, branches curving inward toward some invisible center. Selene spent her seventieth birthday beneath one such tree, where memories of a future not yet lived washed through her—knowledge to be carried, preserved for someone she would never meet.

The spiral never demanded faith. It only needed witnesses to hold space between worlds.

Now, watching her great-granddaughter trace perfect spirals in playground dirt, Selene understands. The child creates not from instruction, but from cellular memory—the same pattern that flows through everything, remembering how to begin again.

§

Appendix (Characters)

Dr. Selene Miro

ROLE: Protagonist. A human biologist specializing in neuro-evolutionary genetics. Mother of a Dawn child.

TRAITS: Brilliant, reserved, emotionally repressed, highly logical, protective.

BACKGROUND: Grew up post-Contact in a world shaped by Virelian-human cooperation. Lost her partner in a mysterious lab accident tied to Dawn development.

MOTIVATIONS: To understand the Dawns on a cellular and cognitive level. Deep down, she hopes to find a way to slow or prevent her child's transformation.

FLAWS: Prone to denial; emotionally detached; subconsciously fears being made obsolete by her own child.

Ansel Miro

ROLE: Selene's 13-year-old child. A first-generation Dawn.

TRAITS: Quiet, otherworldly, unnervingly perceptive, compassionate but unreadable.

ABILITIES: Empathic resonance, regenerative biology, partial non-linear perception.

BACKGROUND: Born through the experimental fusion of Virelian and human genetic material.

MOTIVATIONS: Wants to help humans embrace change, but struggles with alienation from both humans and Virelians.

FLAWS: Torn between his love for his mother and the gravitational pull of an emerging post-human awareness he can barely comprehend.

Virel-Adran

ROLE: Elder Virelian guide and memory-keeper—architect of the recursion cycle and quiet steward of Dawn evolution.

TRAITS: Serene, ancient, metaphorical, emotionally restrained, deeply perceptive, speaks in layered truths.

BACKGROUND: A returning remnant of an older human lineage. Keeper of living archives and recursive lore. Has lived among humans long enough to understand them, but not enough to *be* one.

MOTIVATIONS: To ensure the spiral completes safely. To guide Selene into her role as anchor. To prevent another recursion collapse by helping humanity remember what it once was.

FLAWS: Withholds critical truths. Detached from human grief and attachment. Overconfident in inevitability. Slow to recognize dangers like Burnline. Believes collapse can be a teacher—sometimes at terrible cost.

Commander Ari Kasun

ROLE: Leader of the Earth Sovereign Resistance—anti-integration movement.

TRAITS: Bold, pragmatic, militaristic, sharp-witted, prone to paranoia.

BACKGROUND: Former space force commander. Resigned after witnessing a mass-transformation event she couldn't explain.

MOTIVATIONS: Preserve human sovereignty and ideas

FLAWS: Unable to see the beauty in what she fears. Reacts with aggression when uncertain. Haunted by past failures.

Dr. Lian Penrose

ROLE: Selene's academic rival, now a techno-philosopher aligned with Virelian culture.

TRAITS: Visionary, arrogant, poetic, spiritual.

BACKGROUND: Originally worked with Selene on Dawn neurobiology, but became a public figure advocating for full cultural assimilation into Virelian models.

MOTIVATIONS: Believes humanity must evolve or perish. Views resistance as selfishness.

FLAWS: Seeks transcendence over connection. Will sacrifice ethics for progress.

www.ingramcontent.com/pod-product-compliance
Lightning Source LLC
LaVergne TN
LVHW010638110826
845149LV00014B/2874